HIS BROKEN QUEEN

SOLD TO THE MAFIA BOSS SERIES

ELLA JADE

His Broken Queen © 2022 Ella Jade

Cover Designer: Dark City Designs

Photographer: Eric Battershell

Cover Model: Johnny Kane

All rights reserved under the International and Pan-American Copyright Conventions. No part of this book may be reproduced or transmitted in any form or by any means, electronic or mechanical, including photocopying, recording, or by any information storage and retrieval system, without permission in writing from the publisher.

This is a work of fiction. Names, places, characters and incidents are either the product of the author's imagination or are used fictitiously, and any resemblance to any actual persons, living or dead, organizations, events or locales is entirely coincidental.

Warning: the unauthorized reproduction or distribution of this copyrighted work is illegal. Criminal copyright infringement, including infringement without monetary gain, is investigated by the FBI and is punishable by up to 5 years in prison and a fine of $250,000.

http://authorellajade.com/

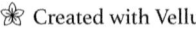 Created with Vellum

CHAPTER 1

Luciana

The crowded club filled to capacity. The music blared out of the speakers as attractive men and sexy women sweat all over one another. The bar was five deep, but that didn't deter thirsty club-goers from waiting for an overpriced drink. Customers tossed hundred-dollar bills in the tip jars as others threw down their credit cards to pay off their expensive tabs.

Anyone who was anyone in the privileged club-scene was here. In the past few months, Cantino's had become the *it* place. If you weren't posting on social media that you were inside these walls, you might as well not post anything at all. People waited hours for a chance to get in. The VIP lists were filled four weeks out. And if it happened to be a night like tonight, when both Romero and Gio were here, word of mouth spread fast. Women would stand outside with their phones ready to record just to get a glimpse of the dangerous and powerful brothers.

As my husband spoke to an associate across the room, several women doubled back, pretending to take selfies, but they weren't fooling anyone. They were trying to get a picture of him to post on their feeds. I'd read some of their captions. Almost all of them hoped they would become his side-piece.

With one sexy glance from him in my direction, he had dashed about twenty of those women's hopes and dreams. Gio would have to pick up the slack. I endured the social media comments and nasty glances from the desperate women because I knew where Romero slept every night.

Two months ago, I escaped my brutal family. Romero rescued me from their twisted world. Some might say I jumped out of the frying pan and into the flame. But if my husband was the flame, I'd gladly burn.

The private area behind the dance floor, known as the *Bilotti* room, buzzed with excitement. Several of Romero's business associates joined us. Gio sat at a table in the corner with his flavor of the week, prominently situated on his lap. Stella and her husband, Mike, sat at a table in the corner, enjoying the vibe of the hottest club in the city. Most of the guys from the house were here too, keeping a watchful eye on us as we celebrated.

"There's the birthday girl." Romero engulfed me in his hold. "Are you having fun?"

"This is all so amazing." I draped my arms over his shoulders. "I've never had a birthday party before."

"You should be celebrated every day." When he pressed his lips to mine, his solid body rubbed against me. "Where's your champagne?"

"It's coming."

"Where's Aria?" He gazed round the room. "I told her the champagne should flow all night. Your glass should never be empty."

"I can wait."

"You shouldn't have to wait." He pulled me closer to him and swayed me to the music. "I'm the owner and you're the guest of honor. We don't wait."

I glided my lips along his jaw, breathing in his spicy scent. He was as sexy as ever tonight. Romero knew how to wear a suit, but he especially knew how to wear one without a tie.

"Are you trying to distract me?" He took my chin between his fingers and lifted my face to meet his. "It's working."

"Good." When I licked my lips, he wasted no time slipping his tongue inside my mouth and kissing me as if no one else was in the room.

I gripped his biceps for stability, as I allowed myself to get lost in his possessive touch.

"Mmm..." I steadied myself against him. "As much as I love this party, I'm ready to go home."

"We haven't had the cake yet, and I might have another surprise for you." He glanced at his watch before whispering into my ear. "There will be plenty of time for me to fuck you later."

I gazed into his eyes, trying to think of a snappy comeback, but I couldn't argue with his statement. I was too mesmerized by the thought of him doing all sorts of wicked things to me.

"I know what you're thinking." He smirked, "Trust me, baby, I've been thinking about it since you came out of the bedroom wearing this alluring dress. I can't wait to get you out of it."

"Well, only because you said there would be cake that I'll be patient." I trailed my lips along his jaw. "But cake will only get you so far."

"You keep enticing me and we'll skip the cake." He

grabbed my backside as he lowered his lips to mine. "I wouldn't plan on walking much tomorrow if I were you."

"Is that a promise?" I bit my lip.

"More like a threat." He winked.

"What are you two discussing?" Stella asked as she and Mike approached us. "Do I want to know?"

"Probably not." Romero hugged her. "We're so glad you both could make it tonight."

"I wouldn't have missed it." Stella took my hand. "You look incredible."

"So do you." I glanced at Mike who seemed to be a little overwhelmed in this environment. Stella told me he was a play-by-the-rules accountant who didn't understand Romero's world. I couldn't blame him. I lived it and I didn't always understand it. "Are you having a good time?"

"We are," she said. "Everything is fantastic."

"I agree." Mike held up his drink. "I might need another."

"I'll walk you to the bar." When Romero placed his arm around Mike's shoulders, Mike jumped. "You look like you could use another drink."

"Be gentle with him." Stella laughed.

"I'll be back soon." Romero kissed my cheek. "I'll make sure you get your champagne too."

"Thank you." I kissed him. "Hurry back."

"You can count on it." When Romero smirked, I knew he was thinking about me not walking tomorrow.

"Is Mike okay?" I asked.

"He's fine." Stella set her glass down on the table. "He's not used to so many large, intimidating men in one room."

"You get used to it." I looked around. "Romero is sitting on a gold mine here."

"Mike said that too."

"Wouldn't it be something if he could leave everything else behind and run this place full-time?"

"Instead of his full-time job?" She glanced in Romero and Gio's direction. They were huddled in the corner, probably talking about that other business. "Do you think he's capable of being a legit businessman?"

"I think he's capable of anything he puts his mind to, but he'll never relinquish the control he has in his world."

As much as I wished we could walk away from this life, I'd come to terms with the revelation that Romero becoming untangled with organized crime wasn't an option. The club was a safe place in my thoughts. If we had this, maybe we could break free one day.

"How does that make you feel?"

"As long as I have him, I don't care what he does for a living."

"He absolutely adores you. I've never seen him so happy."

"I've never been this happy either."

"You both deserve it." She hugged me. "I love how he lights up when he sees or talks about you. Be good to one another."

"We will."

"I better go rescue my husband."

"Thank you for being here." I hugged her a little longer, hoping she knew how much I needed and appreciated her. "It means so much."

"Where else would I be?"

As Stella walked away, Aria joined me with a fresh bottle of champagne. I looked around for Romero, but he seemed to have disappeared into the crowd. I didn't know Aria well, but there was something off about her. She gave me a weird vibe. Almost as if she didn't like me.

"Your impatient husband said your glass shouldn't be empty." She poured some into my flute. "Are you having a good time?"

"Yes." I sipped the champagne. "Thank you."

"Well, you are the guest of honor." She placed the bottle in an ice bucket at the end of my table. "Although, there doesn't appear to be many of your friends or family here. Mostly Romero's muscle and some of his associates."

How observant of you.

"Stella is my friend and Romero and Gio are my family."

"Hmm…" She pressed her full red lips together, gazing around the club. "I guess Romero likes to keep things tight."

"He's selective about the company he keeps." I looked around. "He must be pleased with you. This place is a huge success." I hated to compliment her, but I couldn't deny how well Cantinos was doing.

"Yeah." She ran her fingers through her silky hair, tossing it in my direction. "I need to *persuade* him to pay me more. Don't you think so?"

"How are you going to do that?" I asked. "Persuade him?"

"I have my ways." She smiled. "I'm sure you do as well."

"Yes, but my ways are a lot different from yours." *You do realize I'm his wife.*

"Maybe." She shrugged. "You never know."

"The only reason you're here is because you make my husband money."

"Did he tell you that?"

"I know him better than anyone, and as long as you serve a purpose he'll keep you around." I really didn't like this woman. "Unless you upset me."

"Oh, I serve many purposes."

Before we could finish this conversation, there was a

commotion on the other side of the dance floor. Romero's guards moved to stand next to me as people took out their phones and snapped pictures. I stood on my toes to see over the crowd of people.

"No way," Aria said. "Do you know how good this is for business tonight?"

"What is it?" I tried to figure out what all the fuss was about.

"It looks like you do have family after all." She pointed as Rocco and Sandro walked toward us. "Aren't they your cousins?"

"Ah, yeah, but I don't know why they would be here?"

Both men looked attractive in their designer suits and expensive shoes. Their guards stayed two paces behind them, but the security presence was obvious. People stopped dancing as the two made their way to the private area. There were several celebrities in the club tonight, but no one made an uproar over them. For such a legitimate club, the mafia royalty couldn't be denied.

I hadn't spoken to Rocco since that night Romero rescued me from my uncle and Vincent. I kept in touch with Sandro through text, but I didn't mention the party because I was certain Romero wouldn't want him here.

Did my family have to pick my birthday to send a message?

"Hey, Lu." Sandro moved toward me, but the guards stepped in front of me. "Whoa." Sandro held up his hands. "We're not here to cause trouble."

"It's okay," I said to Salvi. "They're my cousins."

"We know who they are, Lu, but we have to protect you," Salvi said. "That's our job."

"You want to protect her from us?" Sandro asked. "We're not going to hurt her."

Sandro wouldn't hurt me, but I wasn't sure about Rocco. He might not physically hurt me the way Vincent would, but he could go after my husband.

"Happy Birthday, Luciana." Rocco ignored the two large guys standing in front of me and gave me a hug. "I hope you're having a good time."

"I, I am." I took a deep breath before spotting Romero heading our way. "I didn't expect to see you here. I don't want any trouble."

"Neither do we." Sandro stood next to Rocco. "We're not here to ruin your party."

"I'm glad to hear that." Romero forced his guards away with his imposing form so he and Gio could stand on either side of me. "I want my wife's night to be perfect."

They only way it could be perfect is if no one gets shot.

CHAPTER 2

Romero

Luciana gripped my arm, trying to keep me close to her. It looked as if my little surprise may have caused her some stress.

"Rocco, Sandro," I extended my hand. "I'm glad you could join us."

"You invited them?" Lu let out a breath as I shook their hands.

"It's your birthday." I kissed her. "I made an exception."

"Thank you." Her smile spread across her face and that was all the gratitude I needed. Well, at least until I got her into bed. "That means a lot."

"I've missed you." She hugged Sandro.

"I miss you too." He kissed the top of her head. "More than I thought possible."

"Why didn't you tell me you were coming?" Lu asked.

"It was a surprise." Rocco glanced at me. "Did it work?"

"Oh, I'm surprised." Lu tossed a shocked look in my direction. "I never expected this."

"That's why it's a surprise." I looked at my guys. "You can disperse," I said to Salvi. "Everything is fine."

They left to rejoin the party, but Gio stayed behind.

"How have you been?" Lu asked her cousins.

"The firm is really busy," Sandro said. "We do miss our favorite paralegal."

"I'm sure." Lu rolled her eyes. "I've started classes to finish my degree."

"That's wonderful." Rocco nodded. "I wish you nothing but the best."

"Thanks." I could tell Lu was conflicted. I didn't blame her. She was right to be cautious. I was. They were Torrios after all.

"This place is amazing." Sandro looked around the club. "It's all anyone talks about. We haven't been here yet."

"It's supposed to be a legitimate venture, but appearances like mine and yours are making it more popular than I could have imagined," I said. "I don't know if that's a blessing or a curse."

"It's probably pretty popular with the Feds too." Rocco gazed around the room. "That can't be good."

"It has its disadvantages," Gio said. "But we deal with it."

"Let's go get a drink." Sandro took Lu's hand. "We can catch up."

"Okay." Lu smiled at me before Sandro whisked her away.

Inviting Rocco and Sandro was the right move. I battled with my ego, but I wanted my wife to be happy.

"Thanks for coming," I said to Rocco. "Luciana appreciates it."

"I don't think she'll ever forgive me," he said. "My family was horrible to her."

"She's tough." Gio stared at Luciana as she made her

way to the bar. This was the first time Gio and Rocco were together since we found out Rocco could possibly be our sibling. "She has a great life now, thanks to my brother."

"I didn't like the idea of the arrangement between our families. I thought it was too much for Lu to handle," Rocco said. "I thought we were throwing her to the wolves."

"You did." I laughed. "But it turned out to be the right thing for her. I'll always protect her."

"And it turned out well for you, brother." Gio slapped my back. "She makes you a better man."

"I can't argue that." I shrugged. "I needed her."

"Speaking of brothers." Rocco softened his stance. "I have a favor to ask one of you, but I understand if you're not willing to help me."

"What is it?" He piqued my interest.

"I'm ready to take a DNA test," he said. "I could ask my father to provide a sample to prove that we are not a match, but that wouldn't tell me who I am. If one of you were to do it, I'd know for sure."

"You want to know if you're a Bilotti." I glanced at Gio. "Is that something you're really ready for?"

"I need to know who I am." He tightened his jaw. "No matter what I find out."

His admission wasn't easy.

"That's understandable." I didn't envy his position. He was raised as a Torrio, but now his whole life could be blown apart. "I would want to know where I came from too."

"I'll do it," Gio said. "I'll provide the sample."

I nodded my approval.

"Thank you," Rocco said. "I know I'm not your favorite person."

"Let's see what the test results say." I looked across the

dance floor to find Agent Morgan heading my way. "What the hell?"

"What?" Gio followed my gaze. "What does he want?"

As Carson got closer, Rocco said, "Has he been harassing you?"

"He's pissed at us because he can't make any charges against us stick." Gio shook his head. "He needs to move on. Find another target. We're not going to make him famous."

Unless we kill him.

"As long as we're making money in the city, he's not going to leave us alone." If he tried to ruin Luciana's night, I would kill him. "I don't need this tonight. Santino's out of town."

"I can help you," Rocco said. "Tell him I'm your attorney. I'll back him off tonight."

"It's not a bad idea." Gio shrugged. "If it gets him out of here."

I wasn't certain I liked the idea, but before I could answer, Carson was in our space.

"Well, look at this." Carson smirked. "The Bilotti brothers and the Torrio brothers in the same place at the same time. Should the innocent by-standers be concerned when the fall-out happens?"

"There won't be any trouble," I assured him. "I'm married to his cousin, remember?"

"Oh, right, the arranged marriage." Carson looked around. "Where is your beautiful wife? I'd like to say happy birthday to her."

"I'll relay the message." I glared at him. "No need for you to hang around."

"I'd like to stay and ask you a few questions," Carson said. "It shouldn't take too long."

"Anything you have to ask us can wait until tomorrow."

Gio motioned toward the exit. "Why don't you reach out to our attorney in the morning?"

"I hear he's out of town." Carson focused on me. "That is unfortunate for you."

"It would be if I didn't have another attorney." I looked at Rocco. "Can you handle this?"

"No problem," Rocco said. "Agent Morgan, why don't we go to the lobby where it's more private. I'm certain I can answer any questions you may have about this totally legitimate establishment."

"When did you start representing Mr. Bilotti?" Carson asked.

"Is that a relevant question?" Rocco pointed toward the lobby. "You heard him, I'm his attorney now, and I'll handle any inquiries you have while Mr. Marchelli is out of town."

"He's smooth," Gio said as Rocco and Carson walked away. "He could be an asset."

"Maybe if we weren't at war with his family."

"What if he turns out to be a Bilotti? Then he would be our family."

"Let's wait for the test results and then we'll make some decisions."

"Is everything okay?" Luciana joined us. "I saw Carson."

"Just the usual harassment," I sighed. "Rocco is handling it."

"He is?"

"Santino is out of town. I needed an attorney."

"You're full of surprises tonight."

"I'll do whatever it takes to make you happy." I brought her closer to me. "There is nothing I won't do for you."

"Can you get rid of her?" Lu muttered under her breath when Aria made her way toward us.

"What's wrong?" I took her hand. "What did she do?"

"Nothing."

"Would you rather I ask her?" I gritted my teeth. "What did she do?"

"I don't like her."

"Neither do I."

"Romero." Aria touched my bicep. "I'm glad to see you finally found your wife. She looked a little lost a while ago."

"Aria," Gio said. "Why don't you manage the front of the house tonight? The staff you have with us tonight are doing a fantastic job."

"Don't be silly." She took the bottle of champagne out of the bucket and refilled Luciana's glass. "I want to make sure Lu's night is memorable."

"I've already made sure of that." When I took Luciana's face between my hands, Aria's overfilled lips lost their smile. "Baby, I have one more thing that I've been meaning to do for quite a while." I gently kissed her lips. "Now seems like the perfect time."

"Promise you won't be long?" When she licked her lips, my cock stirred. "I'll miss you."

"This won't take long." I released her. "Aria, I need a minute with you."

"Anything you need, I'm your girl." She fluttered her eyelashes at me before smirking at Lu.

You're going to pay for that.

"Sandro," I said. "Would you mind keeping my girl company for a few minutes?"

"Not at all." Sandro took Lu's hand. "Let's go dance."

"Ah…okay." Lu nodded. "Why not?"

"Have fun." I smiled as they made their way to the dance floor. I caught Salvi's attention and pointed at Lu so he knew to keep an eye on her while I was away.

He nodded and followed her to the dance floor.

"Gio, can you join me?" *I'm going to need a witness.* "Let's go to the office."

"Sure." My brother followed me as I guided Aria out of the club and to the back office.

"Is this that important that you're going to take me away from the busiest time of the night?" She tried to keep up with me in her ridiculously high heels. "Couldn't this have waited?"

"Some things can't wait." I opened the office door and turned on the light. "But trust me, I've waited long enough for this."

Gio followed us in and closed the door, causing Aria to jump as it shut.

"Why so jumpy?" I asked. "Do we make you nervous?"

"Not at all." She stared into my eyes, trying to stay in control, but I'd be putting an end to that really soon. "What's so important?"

"I've kept you around here all these months because you've made me a fuck-ton of money." I circled her. "Of course, I've paid you more than you're worth too."

"I wouldn't say that," she said. "I work my ass off for you."

"That might be true, but you have a knack for irritating me." I leaned against my desk. "I can tolerate your incessant flirting, and your inappropriate comments about my brother and I because you make us money, but I have my limits."

"I have no idea what you're talking about." She rolled her eyes. "We haven't interacted that much tonight. I've been too busy making sure your wife's birthday is perfect, remember?"

"Uh oh." Gio smirked. "You really can't read the room, Aria."

"What does that mean?" She fingered the strap of her dress.

"We were talking about my limits." When I moved close to her, she stumbled back, slamming into Gio's chest. "You're right, I wanted my wife's birthday to be perfect, but you couldn't seem to give her that."

"What are you talking about?" She tried to break out from between me and Gio, but we boxed her in. "Her glass was always full, dinner was spectacular, and that overpriced cake you ordered is on its way out." She fidgeted with her hands. "You even invited her cousins to make up for her lack of guests."

"What did you just say?" I placed my hand on top of hers to get her to stop squirming.

"Nothing, I just meant that it didn't seem like she had any friends or family here." She shook her head. "I didn't mean any disrespect. If I hurt her feelings, I'll apologize."

"You said that to Lu?" Gio glanced at me.

"I could tell Lu was uncomfortable around you and I figured you said something to upset her. I thought you might have made an inappropriate comment about me and you." I squeezed her hand. "Do you remember when we first met?"

"Yes."

"I told you not to disrespect my wife." I let go of her hand and gripped her arm. "I've put up with all of your other shit, but I won't allow you to hurt Luciana."

"I didn't mean to." She struggled against me.

"Not ever!" When I yelled, she flinched. "You're done here."

"What?" She pushed against me until I released her. "You can't fire me."

"I think he just did." Gio took her arm. "I'll help you get your things and I'll escort you out."

"You can't do this," she shouted.

"I can do whatever the fuck I want to do in this town." I reached into my pocket and took out my wallet. "I don't like you, but I'm going to let you walk out of here." I took out a wad of cash and dropped it at her feet. "Consider that severance pay."

"Screw you." She yanked out of Gio's hold and got in my face. "I'm going to make you pay for this."

"You've got a set of balls." When I took her throat in my hand, she gasped. "What? Is this not how you imagined me choking you?"

She clawed at my hand.

"You've out-served your purpose." I tightened my hold on her neck. "You're going to take that money and leave. I don't want to hear from you again. If you approach my wife or anyone in my organization, it won't be a painless death for you."

As the mascara-laced tears streamed down her cheeks, she trembled under my hold.

"Are we clear?"

She nodded.

"No." I let go of her throat. "I want to hear you say it, so I know you fucking understand."

"Yes." She gasped for air.

"Yes, what?" I gritted my teeth.

"I won't approach anyone in your family."

"Good." I stepped on the cash I had thrown at her feet on my way out. "Gio, make sure this piece of trash leaves."

"Consider it done," my brother said as I left the office.

I put up with Aria much longer than I had intended to, but

she served a purpose. She ran the club, handled the day-to-day stress, and brought in a lot of money. She could be replaced. I might have tolerated her for longer, but when I saw how Luciana reacted when she had approached us, that was all the motivation I needed to end my association with her. If she was willing to disrespect my wife, she could not be trusted.

As I made my way across the club and to the area behind the bar, the cake was being wheeled out. Rocco walked by my side.

"How did it go?" I asked.

"Morgan is out for blood," he said. "I'd keep my eye on him if I were you."

"It's being handled." I extended my hand as Lu approached us. "There's my girl."

"I thought you were going to miss the cake." Her eyes widened when they brought out the large cart with the massive monarch butterfly cake that I had custom made for her. "Oh God!" She laughed. "You didn't."

"Of course I did."

I kissed her as everyone gathered around the cart. When Stella snapped a picture of the two of us, I winked at her.

"Happy Birthday, my sweet Luciana," I said.

"I love you."

"I love you too, my little butterfly."

CHAPTER 3

*L*uciana

I hurried up the stairs and to our room, still buzzing from the magical evening. Romero followed me as I went on about the party.

"That cake!" I plopped on the bed and dangled my feet over the edge until my shoes hit the floor. "It was gorgeous. I didn't want them to cut it."

Romero smiled at me as he took off his watch, and then set it along with his wallet on the dresser. When he unbuttoned his shirt, I propped myself on my forearms to take in the view of his sculpted chest and chiseled shoulders.

"Thank you for making my birthday so special."

"It's not over yet."

He removed his gun from the back of his pants and set it on top of the dresser. No matter how many times I'd seen him do that, a thrill of excitement coursed through me. It reminded me of how dangerous he was. That danger should have frightened me, but lately all it did was arouse me.

As I continued to gawk at him, he took off his shoes and socks and placed them by the closet. I sat up when he came toward me. Stepping in front of me, he undid his belt buckle. When he popped the button on his pants another surge of arousal shot through my body, pulsating between my legs.

"You're so beautiful." He took my chin between his fingers. "The most beautiful woman in the club tonight."

"I was the luckiest woman in the club tonight." I kissed his fingers when he ran them along my lips. "I was with you."

"No, Lu." He kissed me so softly that it made my heart flutter. "I have you. I'm the lucky one."

"We're both lucky." I reached for the zipper on his pants. "Maybe we should get lucky together."

"That's not a bad idea." He stepped back, giving me enough room to slip off the bed and drop to my knees in front of him. "What are you doing?"

"Showing my gratitude for my birthday party." I licked my lips before grasping his erection in my hand. "Will you let me?"

"Go for it." He glided his fingers through my locks, massaging my scalp as I swirled my tongue over his tip. "Fuck." He tugged on my hair, granting me access to take more of him. "Damn it, Lu." When he forced his hips forward, I placed one hand on his tight thigh, bracing myself for his welcomed assault on my mouth.

I kept pace with him, licking and sucking, making sure to relax when he deep-throated me. The pressure in my core grew with each powerful pass of his hard cock between my lips. My saliva seeped from the corners of my mouth when he pressed his balls against my chin.

His painful grip on my hair only fueled my desire to please him. His moans turned to grunts when I scraped my teeth along his shaft.

"You're going to make me come." He stilled inside my mouth. "As much as I want to watch you swallow, the urge to fuck you is stronger." He pulled out of my mouth and stepped back, holding out his hand for me. "Get up."

I took his hand and let him help me into a standing position. My head swirled from all the birthday champagne. I giggled when I stumbled forward. He caught me in his arms, laughing when my cheeks filled with red.

"Still celebrating?" He ran the back to his fingers along my jaw, causing a hot shiver to channel through me. The fact that my panties were wet and I ached for his touch didn't help matters.

"I love celebrating with you." I swiped my tongue along his lips. "Didn't you say you wanted to fuck me?"

"Such a vulgar mouth." He tugged on my bottom lip. "Was it my cock that made it so filthy?"

"Yes."

"Take your dress off." He let go of me and stepped back. "Now."

I crossed my arm over my chest and slipped the strap of the dress down my shoulder. I did the same to the other side, causing my breasts to spill out of the top. I gazed up at him and smiled.

"Why don't you take it off?"

"Because I told you to do it." He toyed with the buckle on his belt. "Unless you're feeling defiant."

"You'd punish me on my birthday?" I reached under my dress and tugged my panties down, taking them off and tossing them at him. "You take my dress off."

He spun me around and lowered the zipper before I even had a chance to process his actions. He yanked the silky material down my body and let the dress drop to my feet. Grabbing my waist, he tugged me to his chest, pushing his erection against my backside.

"Still feeling disobedient?" He slithered his hand to my center, spreading me open with his fingers. "It's your birthday. How do you want this to go?"

"I don't care how it goes." I moaned when he inserted his fingers in my slick heat. "As long as it ends with you inside me."

As he fingered me, he moved his other hand to my breast, squeezing it in his firm hold. "It was always going to end that way, baby."

"What are we waiting for?" I turned around. "I want you right now."

He kissed my neck, moving to my breasts, kissing them as he cupped one in his hand, biting just above my left nipple.

"Mmm…" I moaned when he reached between us and took his erection in his hand, pushing the tip against my entrance. I hitched my leg over his hip, wiggling into him. As he lifted me up, I wrapped my legs around his waist before hitting the wall behind us.

"Happy Birthday, Luciana." He entered me with one powerful shove of his pelvis.

I held onto his shoulders, keeping my legs hooked tight as he pounded into me. The harder he thrust, the more I wanted. I could hardly catch my breath, but it didn't matter. As long as I could feel all of him inside me, I didn't need to breathe.

He pinned my hands above my head, taking me deeper as he held me captive in his strong hold.

"Oh." I bit my lip as I gripped his hands.

"Scream." He knocked me into the wall. "Let this whole house know what I'm doing to you."

"Romero," I yelled out. "I'm going to…"

I closed my eyes and shuttered into his movements. As I climaxed, he continued to push inside me, claiming me, owning me, loving me the way only he could.

"God!" he yelled out, halting his actions and releasing inside me.

He kissed me slowly as he emptied into me. When I opened my eyes, I found him staring at me.

"What?" I gently kissed him.

"Nothing." He lowered me to my feet, steadying me by holding me close to him. "It's just that you're the most stunning woman I've ever known. You're sweet, kind, and tender. Sometimes, I don't know what you're doing with me."

"Seriously?" I laughed. "Remember how we met?"

"Okay, I did force you to marry me, but you didn't have to fall in love with me."

"I didn't have a choice." I traced the tattoos along his chest with my finger. "That was the easy part."

"I don't deserve you, but I'll prove I can be the man you need."

"You don't have to prove anything."

The past couple of months had been quiet, but lately, I saw a change in my husband. Something was weighing heavily on his mind. He and Gio had more closed-door meetings than usual, and Romero ramped up security around the house.

He glanced at the dresser when his phone buzzed with a message. "I have to see who that is." He let go of me and pulled up his pants. "We can take a shower."

"Sounds good." I let go of his hand as he reached for his phone. "Is everything okay?"

"I have to call Gio back."

"Where did he disappear to tonight? He wasn't there when we cut the cake."

"We had something to deal with. He's still at the club."

"How come?"

"He's the new manager for the time being."

"Wait? What happened to Aria?" Just mentioning her name made me sick. I didn't like the way she spoke to me tonight, and I definitely didn't like how she insisted she was an asset to my husband.

"She's no longer useful to me, so I fired her."

"You did?" I couldn't say I was upset about that.

"You don't have to hide your satisfaction." He ushered me into the bathroom and turned on the shower. "I know you don't like her."

"I barely know her." But he was right, I was happy she was gone.

"She upset you tonight and that couldn't go unanswered."

"You fired her because she upset me?"

"It seemed like a good enough reason."

"Oh."

"I didn't trust her before, but after I saw how uncomfortable she made you, she had to go." He pointed to the shower stall. "I'll join you in a few minutes. Let me call Gio back."

"I hope this management change doesn't cause extra stress for you." I sensed he had already been dealing with so much even if he couldn't tell me what was going on.

"You let me worry about it. No one disrespects my wife."

"Thank you." I stepped under the stream of the multiple shower heads. "Aria did make me feel uncomfortable. She tried to make me believe she had a chance with you. As if." I rolled my eyes. "I know better."

"I'm glad." He glanced at my body and licked his lips. "I won't be long."

"I hope not or I'll have to find other ways to occupy myself while I'm in here." I ran my hand over my breasts and down my stomach.

"Be careful." He gripped my wrist. "I might make you do that while I watch."

"Hurry back."

He groaned as he left the bathroom to tend to his business. I was used to him taking care of urgent matters at all hours of the day and night, but over the last few days it seemed to be happening more frequently.

Ever since we broke away from my family, we had been living as if nothing could touch us. I believed it when he said everything was fine, but I knew better. Nothing was ever fine in this world. A world where men like my husband, uncle, and cousins killed for what they deemed important.

The sad truth was men like them could disappear in a heartbeat defending what they thought was important. This life of loyalty, honor, and respect could be deadly.

CHAPTER 4

Romero

"Gio, I don't want to hear anymore fucking bad news." I squeezed the bridge of my nose. "We haven't moved product in months. Our contacts are drying up. I'm useless to the cartel now."

"If it's any consolation," Gio said. "No one is moving anything. It's not just us. The Torrios are still recovering from the hit they took when we blew up the warehouse. The cartel doesn't trust them either. The other families are laying low because they're worried we're going to go to war with the Torrios and no one wants to choose sides. Plus, the Feds are putting a lot of pressure on all of us."

"I didn't want this involvement." I slammed my fist on my desk. "The fucking Torrios caused all of these problems for us."

"You did get Lu out of the deal."

I looked up from my laptop.

"Where do we stand with her new guard?" Salvi was doing double duty and that only worked because I didn't let Luciana leave the house without me. She only agreed to that because she was busy with her online courses, but she needed her own guard.

"I did what you asked me to do, but I don't know if it's going to work out or if it would be considered in poor taste to take a guard from one family, especially that family, and put him in ours. How do we know we can trust him?"

"It's the right move."

"What about Jag?"

"Don't." I held up my hand. "That piece of shit almost got my wife killed. The only reason he's still breathing and employed with us is because you like him. I will not trust him with her ever again."

"We are short staffed if you haven't noticed." Gio tapped his fingers on the edge of my desk. "I'm vetting security as fast as I can, but I don't trust a lot of the guys coming our way. They have too many ties to other families. Given the circumstances of the last mole in this house, I can't take any chances."

I glared at him.

"Hey, I love Lu too, but we have to be smart about who we let in here." He gazed out the window. "Not to mention, with Giancarlo gone and Santino out of the country, we don't have any advisors."

"We don't need advisors."

"We need eyes and ears everywhere." He sighed. "And now that I'm running the club, I have to split my focus. I'm not comfortable with that. We're in a vulnerable position."

"Is there anyone at the club we can trust to run things? Aria didn't do everything by herself."

"There is the accountant. She seems to know what she's doing."

"That shy little thing who scurries every time we enter the building?"

"She's not that shy and can you blame her for getting out of our way?" He shrugged. "At least you don't have to worry about her throwing herself at you every time you show up."

"I guess it could work." I made a note in my club file. "What's her name?"

"Lara Cirrico. She's Italian."

"Have her shadow you. See if she can handle the responsibility until we can find a replacement. Tell her we'll compensate her for her troubles." I glanced at my watch. "Any word on Aria?"

"She's been making noise this morning. Trying to find a new job and trashing us around town. It's nothing I can't handle."

"If she gets too loud, make sure she's silenced."

"I don't think she'll be a problem after a few days."

"You know your priorities?"

"Do you have to ask?" He gave me the finger. "Lu's guard is top priority. I know that."

"I'm sorry." I shook my head. "Ever since Vincent took her so easily that day, I can't forgive myself. I never should have let her go to the city without me."

"It wasn't your fault."

"Has that son of a bitch resurfaced?" We hadn't seen Vincent since the night I left with Luciana.

"He's still hiding from us, but they will never admit that," Gio said. "I'm surprised Sandro and Rocco showed up last night."

"Sandro did it for Luciana." I clasped my hands together. "Rocco came to protect his brother."

"From us?"

"You don't think so?"

"I kind of got the feeling he thought we were his brothers too."

"No, he wants that DNA test to prove we're not his brothers. That would make all of our lives so much easier."

"He stepped in and helped us last night." Gio tightened his lips. "He didn't have to do that. Carson could have pulled you out of there without Santino around. We could be facing another headache today if not for Rocco."

"Where's this loyalty coming from? He was complicit on the whole marrying off Luciana plan. He had no problem spying on us. He also didn't give us a heads up when Vincent took her."

"Why would he?" Gio asked. "He was a Torrio then. He might be a Bilotti now."

"It's another complication we don't need. It's bad enough that my wife is related to them. Do you really think we need one more of their family members?"

"What if he's an asset?"

"Let's wait for the results of the test and then we'll decide." I checked my watch again. "I have to go."

"Where?"

"It's Luciana's real birthday today." I had plans to take her to a quiet dinner and give her a birthday gift. "Last night was overwhelming for her."

"She had a great time."

"She did, but that was more my speed. The club, the crowds, the cake. Tonight, she deserves a low-key evening with just the two of us."

"You're such a fucking romantic, who knew?" He laughed. "I'll be at the club looking for someone to fuck. No romance."

"You're a real prince." I threw a pen at him.

"Maybe I just haven't found my queen yet."

"When you do, you'll know and your life will never be the same again." *Trust me.*

As we drove down the back road on the way to our house, Luciana couldn't stop staring at the charm that dangled from the bracelet I had given her a couple of months ago. Tonight, I added her first charm. A diamond butterfly.

"Do you like it?" I took her hand.

"I love it." She squeezed my hand. "You didn't have to get me anything. The party last night. Dinner tonight. It's too much."

"Not when it comes to you." I kissed her knuckles. "I want to give you the world."

"You already have." She glanced out the window. "Is that Joey in front of us?"

"Yeah." I motioned toward the car behind us. "I have someone following too. You're precious cargo."

She tightened her hold on my hand.

"What's wrong?"

"Salvi is with us." She pointed to the driver's seat. "Joey is in front of us and a guard behind us. What's going on?"

"Nothing, I'm being cautious."

"If we have an entourage, who is guarding the house?"

"There are a few guys at the house." I ran my finger along her wrist. "But, they don't have much to do tonight since we're not home."

"When can I get Jag back?" She bit her lip.

"We've talked about this."

"No, you've talked about it and I listened."

"That's the way I like it."

"Romero?"

"Lu, Jag is not a good fit for you." With some factors of my business being out of my control, I wasn't taking any chances with my wife. "I'll find someone else for you."

"I don't want someone else." She let go of my hand and placed hers in her lap, which infuriated me, but I didn't want to fight with her on her birthday. "I need to go to the library tomorrow. I want Jag to take me."

"No."

"No, Jag can't take me or I can't go to the library?"

"Jag can't take you, but Salvi can."

"He is supposed to protect you, right, Salvi?"

Salvi glanced at me in the rearview mirror, but he knew better than to say anything, or he would go a few rounds with me.

"Don't put him in the middle," I said. "It's not fair."

"Is it fair to make Jag wash the cars and clean the pool?"

"It's October, we closed the pool."

"You know what I mean." She pressed her sexy lips together. "It wasn't his fault what happened. I told him to park the car. I got out before he could stop me."

"It's his job to make sure you don't do stuff like that." I clenched my fist. "I'd appreciate it if you didn't do stuff like that. Not now."

"What does that mean?"

"I want to keep you safe, and I can't do that if you don't listen to your guard." I tightened my jaw when I thought how things could have gone if I didn't get to her after her family took her. What would Vincent and his witch of a mother have done to her? "Jag doesn't have control over you. You don't respect him."

"That's not true."

"You view him as a friend."

"That bothers you?"

"He can be your friend while he washes the cars. He's not going to be responsible for your life. End of story."

She opened her mouth to say something but thought better of it. She wasn't going to win this battle.

"I don't want to fight with you." I unbuckled my seatbelt and moved closer to her as Salvi followed Joey into the driveway. "You just have to trust me, okay?"

"I do," she whispered. "Even if I don't understand it."

"Everything I do is to keep you safe." I pressed my lips to hers. "I promise."

She rested her palm against my cheek.

"Boss?" Salvi opened his car door when we got to the house. "Something's not right."

I glanced out the window to see Joey headed toward the house with his gun already drawn.

"What the hell?"

The front door was wide open but none of the other guards were around.

"What's wrong?" Lu unbuckled her seatbelt. "The door is open."

Salvi drew his gun and followed Joey.

I reached for my piece before turning to Luciana. "Stay here." I motioned behind me. "The guys behind us will guard the car."

The two guards who were following us got out and came to my side of the car.

"Don't leave my wife," I said. "No matter what happens."

"Why is Stella here?" Lu opened her door and headed toward Stella's car before I could stop her. "She's not supposed to be here."

"Luciana," I called after her as I came around the car and followed her up the driveway. "Get back here."

I hurried to catch her from approaching the house. As she made her way to Stella's car, Jag and two other guards came from the direction of the backyard.

"What is happening?" I asked. "Is it secure?"

"Yes, Joey and Salvi are inside now," Jag said. "We heard a shot and then on the camera we saw two men fleeing through the yard. We went after them, but couldn't catch them."

"Where did the shot come from?" When I glanced at Stella's car, dread settled inside my chest.

"Inside the house," Jag said.

"Where's Stella?" Lu headed in the direction of the porch.

"No!" I grabbed her arm.

"Where is she?" She trembled. "Is she inside?"

The other two guards looked at their feet, but when Jag stared into my eyes, his gaze was filled with sorrow.

"No," I whispered.

"What?" Luciana broke out of my hold and ran toward the house. "Stella!"

"Lu!" I chased after her. "Wait!"

As I got to the doorway, Luciana was already inside, but Salvi blocked her way to the kitchen.

"Lu," he said. "You have to wait outside."

I joined them in the foyer.

"The house is secure." Salvi glanced toward the kitchen. "The front door was open when we arrived. I'm going to go pull the footage from the camera."

"Call Gio," I said. "Where's Joey?"

"In the kitchen." He sighed. "It's not good."

"Stella?" Lu ran down the hall. "No!" She dropped to her knees in the archway of the kitchen. "No, no, no!"

CHAPTER 5

Luciana

Joey stood in the doorway, trying to block the bloody scene in front of me, but it was too late. I would never forget the sight of Stella's lifeless body on the floor of the kitchen. She bled from the back of her head. I didn't understand what had happened.

"Luciana." Romero dropped down next to me and wrapped his arms around my shaking form. "We can't stay here." He glanced up at Joey. "We have to get out of here."

"We have to report this one," Joey said. "It's not like the others."

"I know." Romero held me tighter. "It was a home invasion. Lu and I weren't here. The less she has to talk to the cops the better."

A home invasion? Who would dare try to rob the house of an arms dealer? The place was full of security and cameras. Why was Stella here? How did this happen to her?

I could hear Romero talking, but I couldn't process the words. All I could think about was Stella. "Is she cold?" I whispered. "In pain?"

Romero continued to speak to the guys. "Gio will help you get your story together, but mostly you'll say what you told me. You heard a shot."

"Oh." I put my hand over my mouth. "Stella."

"It's okay." He kissed the top of my head.

"No, it isn't," I screamed. "Stella is dead. She's dead." I sobbed into his chest. "Why?"

I lifted my head and stared into the kitchen, bawling harder when I realized I would never get to hear her voice again. We weren't going to have any more conversations as she taught me how to cook. She wouldn't be able to tell me about her girls.

"Her daughters?" I looked at Romero. "Their mom isn't coming home. How are they going to deal with that? Her husband? Her dad? What are we going to do about them?" I couldn't take a deep breath. "Romero." I gripped his shirt in my hand. "I can't breathe."

"Get the doctor here," Romero shouted at someone. "Now."

"I feel sick." I couldn't stop trembling. "I can't catch my breath."

"Try to breathe, baby." He took his suit jacket off and draped it over my shoulders.

"Do you think Stella is cold?"

"No." He turned me to face him, so I didn't have to look into the kitchen. "She's not cold. She's watching you, Luciana. She knows how much you love her."

"I do love her." My chest ached. "I don't want her to not be here anymore. I need her."

"She's going to be with you." He hugged me. "You have me, Lu. I'm here. I'm going to make this right."

"Can you bring Stella back?" I shook my head. "My stomach hurts."

"Are you going to be sick?"

"Maybe." I nodded. "I don't know."

"It's okay." He gently lifted me into his arms and carried me to the stairs. "Can you make it to our bathroom?"

"I think." I put my hand over my mouth as he took me to our bedroom. "Romero, I'm going to throw up."

He rushed us into the bathroom and placed me in front of the toilet.

I heaved as I fell to my knees and gripped the seat. Romero swiped up my hair and held it to the side as I vomited into the bowl.

I retched so hard, my stomach muscles burned.

"It's okay, Lu." He rubbed my back. "I'm here."

He tried to comfort me, but it was far from okay and he knew it. I sat down on the cool tiles, trying to steady my breaths. I couldn't get the image of Stella out of my mind. I began to cry again when I thought about her. She must have been so afraid.

"Why did they kill her?" I whispered.

"I don't know, but I promise you I'll find those cowards and I will make them pay." He stood and extended his hand. "We have to leave."

"Why?"

"Because I can't be caught up in this right now." He guided me into a standing position. "I won't subject you to any questioning. We're going to go back to the city and stay at the penthouse until things settle down with the police."

"I don't want to leave her."

"Baby, it has to be called in. I don't know what time she got here. Her husband will be looking for her soon."

"Why was she here?"

"It doesn't matter."

"It does to me."

His Broken Queen 37

"She brought you a cake." He took my hands in his. "She wanted us to have it when we got back from dinner."

"No." I trembled again. "She wasn't supposed to be here."

"She wanted to be here."

"This is my fault."

"No." He pulled me into an embrace. "You're the last person whose fault this is."

"If she wasn't bringing me a cake on my birthday she would be at home right now." I wanted to scream, but when I opened my mouth, nothing came out. "This isn't fair."

"I'm sorry." He opened the bathroom door. "We have to go."

"I need to brush my teeth and put some water on my face." I let go of his hand. "I need a few minutes alone."

"I'll get us a few things to take to the penthouse." He looked me over. "Do you want to get changed before we go?"

I shook my head.

"Try to be quick."

Once he left the bathroom, I shut the door and leaned against it. My legs wanted to give out and my stomach churned, but I had to pull myself together. I went to the sink and turned on the faucet. The cool water offered little relief as I splashed it on my warm face. Brushing my teeth was no better. Each time the toothbrush hit the back of my throat, my gag reflex kicked in which only made my stomach feel worse. My hands wouldn't stop shaking.

When I glanced in the mirror, I didn't recognize the woman staring back at me. My disheveled hair fell down my face, the black mascara had smeared underneath my eyes, making me look tired, and my lipstick was smudged at the corners of my mouth.

I didn't know pain like this could exist, and I was no

stranger to pain. I was young when my parents died. I remembered crying when I realized they weren't coming back. I grieved for them as a ten-year-old child could, but I didn't fully understand the loss. Not like I do today.

"Lu." Romero knocked on the bathroom door. "Can I come in?"

He didn't wait for me to answer.

"Do you still feel sick?" He flushed the toilet, getting rid of my last episode.

"I'm not going to be sick, but I don't feel good." I wiggled out of his jacket. "One second I'm cold, and the next I'm really hot. My throat is dry and my stomach aches. I want to lie down."

He guided me out of the bathroom and to our bed. I scooted to the middle of the mattress and curled

into a ball, shivering when I closed my eyes. Romero covered me with the throw from the edge of the bed. I didn't know how long I stayed there. It was probably only a few minutes, but time seemed to be moving slower.

Romero stirred around the room, tossing clothes into an overnight bag. We didn't talk. His phone kept buzzing with messages. Did he already know who did this? Was this my family's retaliation? Could my uncle have been so ruthless that he killed an innocent woman?

I shot up into a seated position and glanced around the room.

"Lu." Romero joined me on the bed. "What's wrong?"

"Who did this?"

"I don't know yet." He tucked the hair that had fallen into my face behind my ear. "Dr. Caro is on his way up. He's going to give you something to help you relax."

"Did my uncle do this?"

"I hope not."

The soft knock at the door startled me.

"It's Gio and the doctor." Romero held me close. "Come in."

"I don't need a doctor," I whispered. "I'm fine."

"You can't stop shaking." He pressed his lips to my temple. "Let me take care of you."

"Hey, beauty." Gio came into the room, with a tall, handsome older man behind him. "I brought a friend who can help you."

"I don't need help, but Stella does."

Gio glanced at Romero.

"Luciana," the man who I assumed was the doctor said. "I'm Brett."

I scooted closer to Romero.

"I'm a friend of your husband, and I'd like to help you. How are you feeling?" Brett asked as he set a black bag on the bed.

"Not good," I said. "My head hurts, I'm sick to my stomach, and I'm really cold."

"I can give you something to relax you." He reached into his bag and took out a syringe. "It's mild and it will help you sleep."

"I don't need anything." I looked at Romero. "Can we go see Stella?"

"No, baby." He nodded at the doctor.

"Romero, we have to go," Gio said. "We've waited too long already."

"Too long for what?" I asked.

"We have to have someone come for Stella now." He held me close. "Just relax, okay?"

I glanced over my shoulder as Brett came toward me with the needle.

"I don't need that." I held up my hand, but Romero took

it in his. "I want to see Stella. I have to say goodbye. I have to tell her goodbye." I sobbed. "Please, I don't want to leave her. She's all alone down there."

"No." Romero wrapped his arms around me, pinning mine against my body. "She's not alone, but we have to get her back to her family now."

"Oh, God!" I screamed out. "She's not going home. She won't be able to see her girls ever again. They lost their mom." I couldn't catch my breath. "You have to fix this."

"I will." He stroked my hair. "Close your eyes now."

The needle pierced my skin as I rested my head on Romero's chest. My eyes fluttered and my breathing slowed. It was like the time I had gotten my wisdom teeth out. I was drowsy and weightless. I tried to fight it because I didn't want to leave here, but if I slept for a bit, maybe when I woke up this would all be just a nightmare.

"Let's get her to the car," Gio said.

"What the fuck, Gio." Romero carried me down the hall. "How did this happen?"

I struggled to stay awake, but the drug was strong. Romero looked down at me as he took me down the stairs. "I love you, Lu."

CHAPTER 6

Romero

Gio handed me a glass of vodka as I stared out the penthouse windows. The city lit up the skyline, but the mood here was dark. I was no stranger to death. I'd killed before. Out of revenge, retaliation, betrayal. I'd lost people close to me. The loss of Stella cut deep.

"This is my fault." I sipped the vodka. "I brought her into my house."

"She knew who you were when she agreed to work for you."

"It doesn't matter." I set the glass on the coffee table. "She would still be alive if she wasn't working for me. Lu blames herself, but it's not on her."

"No, it's on the scum who would take out an innocent woman."

"I need to know who did this."

"No one has taken responsibility for it." Gio ran his hand through his hair. "Maybe it was a message gone wrong. Stella wasn't supposed to be in the house."

"I don't care if they weren't supposed to kill her," I shouted. "They fucking did and I'm going to make them suffer."

Stella had been a friend for years. She was loyal and kind. Her devotion and friendship to Luciana would never be forgotten. Her death would not go unanswered.

When the penthouse phone rang, Gio picked it up.

"Yeah, that's fine," he said. "You can send him up."

I glanced at my brother as he hung up.

"Rocco." He finished his drink. "Maybe he'll have some answers."

"He's still a Torrio," I said. "Don't forget that."

Gio went to the door and opened it, saying something to the guard in the doorway. When he returned from the hallway, Rocco was with him.

"Did your family do this?" I stared at him. "Did they send someone to my home to kill a friend to send me a message?"

"I know you have to ask me that and I'm sorry for what happened to Stella, but no," he said. "That's not the way any of the prominent families deal with a situation. None of us would come to your home and kill an innocent woman. The only message that would send is we are savage and have no code. We may do a lot of despicable acts, but we do them to one another. Not to innocent people."

I nodded, satisfied with his answer because he was right. None of the families would stand back and allow such a heinous act to be committed against any of the other members in the organization.

"Agent Morgan is right behind me." Rocco glanced at his phone. "I have someone in the lobby monitoring the situation."

"Just what I fucking need." I poured myself another drink.

"I can take care of him tonight," Rocco said.

"The official story is that Romero and Luciana were not at the scene at all." Gio took the bottle of vodka. "Do you want a drink?"

Rocco waved him off. "I have to stay sharp." He looked at me. "How is Lu?"

"She's sedated right now. She can't talk to the cops. She'll break and say what she saw." I clenched my fist. "She can't help identify the shooter, so I'm not subjecting her to this."

"I can keep Morgan away from her, especially if we say she wasn't home." Rocco glanced at his phone. "Your building security is letting Agent Morgan up. He probably waved his badge."

"Why are you helping us?" I asked. "Your father and brothers aren't going to like it."

"They don't like a lot of things I do these days. What's one more to add to the list?"

Gio went to the door and waited for Morgan to arrive.

"I know you don't trust me," Rocco said. "But things haven't been right in the organization for weeks. The families are split but we have a common enemy and if we don't start working together, it's not going to get any better. No one is moving anything."

"Your father set the cartel in our paths," I reminded him. "I had a working relationship with them before he undermined me."

"I don't know what my father's motivation was when he came after you. I followed his lead because that's what I've always done."

"And now?"

Before he could answer, Gio came in with Morgan.

"Mr. Bilotti," Agent Morgan said. "I take it your night isn't going well."

"Here's a thought, instead of harassing me, why don't look for the people involved with invading my house tonight?" It wasn't as if he was going to find them faster than I could.

"I have a thought too," he said. "How about we cut the bullshit and you tell me who murdered your employee."

"Stella was more than an employee." I walked across the room to stand closer to him. "She was a good friend, especially to my wife."

"How is Lu?" He didn't appear as smug when he mentioned her name.

"I'm taking care of her," I said.

"I'd like to speak with her," he said.

"That's not going to be necessary," Rocco answered before I could. "She wasn't there and she doesn't know anything."

"We'd like to see the footage from your security cameras at your house," Carson said. "It's crucial in this investigation."

"You'll need a warrant for that," Rocco said. "With specific dates. Tonight's footage only."

"Why, Mr. Torrio? Are you afraid we'll find something else?" Carson asked. "I'm sure Mr. Bilotti doesn't have anything to hide."

Carson was baiting me, and of course, he thought a criminal like me wasn't as smart as an educated federal agent.

"These people could have been casing your house for a few days," he said. "You do want to find out who did this, don't you?"

"I'll tell my security team to hand over the last few days of footage," I said. "Will that help?"

"Very much." Carson took out his phone. "I'll head to your house now."

"I'll meet you there," Rocco said. "In case you have any questions."

"I'm sure we'll have plenty of questions." Carson headed to the hallway. "Tell Lu I'm thinking of her."

"Don't think about my wife," I mumbled as he exited the penthouse. "We need to do something about him."

"I can handle him tonight, but if you hand over that footage, it will show you and Lu entering the house. We won't be able to protect her from questioning then."

"It's been taken care of," Gio said. "As far as the Feds are concerned, the cameras were disabled a few days ago. We don't know why. Maybe the burglars did it?"

"That could never happen in my house, but Morgan doesn't need to know that." I took a long sip from my glass, but the alcohol did nothing to relax me. I needed to be close to Luciana.

"Clever," Rocco said, "You're creating a set up for a home invasion."

"They were wearing masks." When I thought about the footage I had seen on my security cameras, I was filled with rage. "There were two of them. They followed Stella in when she brought the cake." I closed my eyes, wishing the vodka would take hold of me. "Luciana can never know Stella knew it was coming."

Rocco and Gio nodded in agreement.

"We need to figure out who sent this message," I said. "The longer it takes, the colder the trail will get."

"I'll call you when I get to your house and let you know what's happening," Rocco said.

"Thank you." I turned and gazed out at the windows, looking down at the bustling city.

When Gio returned from seeing Rocco out, he joined me by the window.

"I'm going to go and check on Luciana." I finished the rest of the vodka in my glass. "Why is she in the master bedroom?"

"I never made the move." He shrugged. "The guest bedroom is fine."

"Why didn't you switch bedrooms when I moved out?"

"I wasn't sure where the marriage thing was going to lead, I guess. Then there was the whole betrayal clusterfuck, and I figured if you didn't kill her, you'd get divorced and come back here."

"I'm not getting divorced." I looked into my empty glass. "I'm not going to kill her either."

"I know." He smiled. "I'm glad you have her."

"Me too." I shook my head. "Even if I do owe the fucking Torrios for that."

"You don't trust Rocco," he said.

"I want a rush on the DNA test." I headed to the hallway. "I can't trust him until I know there's Bilotti blood running through his veins."

~

WHEN I ENTERED THE BEDROOM, the lamp by the bed was on the lowest setting, creating a soft stream of light inside the room. Luciana was curled up in a ball in the exact same position I'd left her in a few hours ago.

After emptying my pockets, I removed my gun, and then took off my shirt. Before getting into bed, I took off my socks and shoes. I didn't plan on staying long. I had too much to sort out, but I needed to hold her.

She rolled over and faced me when the mattresses dropped from my weight, but she didn't open her eyes. Her long hair was tangled and spread out on the pillow. She still had on the blue dress she'd worn to celebrate her birthday. When I took her out tonight, I had imagined we would end up in bed, but I never expected it wouldn't be our bed, and we'd be dealing with a tragedy of epic proportions.

I pulled her onto my chest and held her against me. How was she ever going to forgive me for this? How would I ever forgive myself? My world was dangerous. I knew the risks. I never cared about anyone the way I did for Luciana. With the exception of Gio, everyone in my life was replaceable. Then I met her, and nothing had been the same since.

Lu stirred in my arms. I rubbed her back, trying to lull her back to sleep. She didn't need to be awake now. It would only cause her pain.

"Romero." She sat up, her eyes were groggy and her voice was raspy. "Where are we?"

"The penthouse." I took her hand. "In the city."

"Stella?"

"She didn't make it, baby." I caressed her face. "I'm sorry."

"I hoped it was a dream." A tear streamed down her cheek. "It's a nightmare."

"I wish I could make this all go away." I sat up, and then wiped the tears from her face with my hand. "This isn't the life I want to give you."

"It's your life." She gently touched my lips with her fingertips. "That makes it my life. For better or worse, remember?"

"When you said those vows, you didn't mean them."

"Not then, but I do now."

"You're too good for me." I had known that all along, but there was no way I'd ever let her go.

"I'm yours." She rested her head on my shoulder. "Stella helped me come to terms with our relationship. She told me I needed to forgive myself for what I had done to you. She made me see how much you meant to me."

"She told me on more than one occasion that I needed to forgive you because it wasn't your fault. I knew she was right."

"She was so happy for us." She quietly wept into my neck. "She said she couldn't wait for us to renew our vows so she could see how much we loved one another."

"I'm sorry we haven't done that yet." There was so much going on, but I wanted to give her the wedding she deserved this time. Not the one she was forced into. "I'm sorry we waited."

"Me too." She lifted her head. "Not because I need another wedding, but because I wanted Stella there to stand by my side when I pledge my life and love to you." She sobbed. "Now that's never going to happen."

I pulled her close to me and let her cry. After a while, her breathing returned to normal and she settled down. She trailed her lips along my jaw, working her way to my lips.

"Can you kiss me?" She pressed her lips to mine.

I gave her what she wanted. What we both needed. A safe place to grieve. A connection we both shared. I softly kissed her, lingering at her mouth, wanting to be close to her. I lowered her to the mattress, taking my time kissing her. There was no urgency, just a desire to be in the moment.

She ran her hand down my chest and to the buckle of my belt. I rested my head on the pillow as she took control of the kiss, probing her tongue inside my mouth. She unbuttoned my pants, but when she lowered the zipper, I gripped her wrist.

"No," I whispered. "Not tonight."

"Why not?" She kissed my neck, rubbing her hand along my aroused cock. "I want to."

"You're upset and you're not feeling well," I reminded her. "I can hold you while you rest. I can be here for you."

"I need to be with you." She continued to palm my shaft through my pants. "Please."

I rolled her on her back, and hovered over her. Gliding my hand down her neck, and to her breasts. I kissed her harder than before, trying to push back the lust building inside me, but when she gazed at me with those desperate eyes, I couldn't deny her request.

"You're sure?" I circled my finger over her nipple. "We don't have to."

"I want to." She guided my hand under her dress and to her panties. "I need to feel something other than hurt."

I had never comforted someone with sex before, but then I'd never been in love before. I would do anything for her. If being close to me was what she needed, I would give her that.

She tugged my pants over my hips as I slid her panties down her legs and to her ankles. She kicked out of them so I could hitch her legs around my waist. I pressed my tip against her wet opening, taking my time to ease into her.

She inhaled as I inched inside her. "Romero." She gripped my shoulders as she spread her legs, allowing me full access to her.

Once I was sheathed in her heat, she wrapped her legs around me and moved with me. Slow and steady, in and out.

We created a perfect rhythm, taking our time to feel one another, to appreciate the bond we had created.

When I kissed her, the tears that had dampened her cheeks transferred onto my skin. She took my face between her hands, staring at me with grief-stricken eyes. The sight of her shattered my heart into a million pieces.

"Do you want me to stop?" I asked.

"No." She clasped her legs tighter around my waist. "I need us."

I moved my hands along her sides, gently touching her, taking her soft skin in my firm hold. We continued to progress at a slow pace, pleasing one another quietly, tenderly.

After a few minutes, both of us stopped advancing, taking in the moment. We kissed, touched, and gazed into one another's eyes. The room was silent with the exception of our labored breaths. I thrust one final time, granting each of us the release we so desperately needed. Our simultaneous climaxes were quiet and soft. No thrashing, no screaming, and no mutual nods of bliss. It was fitting for the moment.

I wiped her tears away before rolling off her. I rested onto my side and pulled her back to my chest, holding her close to me. She quietly wept as she trembled against me. How was I ever going to make her whole again?

"I'm sorry, Lu." I didn't know what else to say.

"I don't blame you."

Her admission made my chest ache with sorrow and regret. For the first time since my mother died, I allowed the grief to pour out of me. My heart rate increased and I had trouble taking a deep breath. I closed my eyes, trying to get it together. I couldn't allow myself to fall apart now. I let out a slow breath, wishing I had consumed more vodka to take this pain away.

"Romero," she whispered. "Stella doesn't blame you either."

Fuck! I touched my face with my fingertips, wiping the tears that had fallen from my eyes. I would allow myself this moment of weakness, but after tonight, I would show no mercy to my enemies.

Ruthless didn't begin to describe me.

CHAPTER 7

Luciana

I had showered, changed into a fresh pair of yoga pants and a gray t-shirt, and managed to make my way downstairs. I glanced around at the massive space, squinting as the sun poured in from the large windows that surrounded the living room.

This was Romero's life before he married me. This was where he came when he learned that I had betrayed him. He brought me here to shelter me from what had happened to Stella. This was his safe place. A refuge from his brutal world.

"Lu." Romero stood at the bottom of the stairs. "What are you doing out of bed?"

"I can't stay in bed forever." I took the last few steps and joined him. "We've been here for two days and I haven't left the bedroom."

"You need to rest." He tucked my hair behind my ear. "I can get you whatever you want."

"You keep leaving me." Not leaving the bedroom for a

few days would be intriguing if we were making love all day, but that wasn't the case. "I don't want to be alone."

"I'm sorry. I've been working."

Did that mean he was looking for the men who killed Stella? Did I want to know?

"How are things going?"

"With my work?"

"No, just in general, I guess." The less I knew about this situation, the better I would feel.

"Are you hungry?" He ignored my question.

I shook my head.

"You haven't eaten since yesterday afternoon and you barely ate anything then."

"I don't feel like eating."

"I'll make you tea and toast." He took my hand and led me to the kitchen. "Indulge me and eat something."

"Have you heard from Stella's family?" I sat on the stool at the island. "Can we go and see them?"

"We should leave them alone for now." He put the kettle of water on for the tea. "Can I make you my mom's stuffed French toast?"

"That sounds really good, but I don't want to waste it." I pressed my hand to my stomach. "I'm still uneasy."

"You'll start to feel better soon."

"We should pay our respects to her family," I said. "Don't you think we owe them that?"

"I sent flowers and food." He took a mug from the cabinet next to the stove. "That's enough for now."

"We're going to the funeral, right?"

"We'll talk about that later."

"Why can't we talk about it now?"

"Lu!" When he shouted, I jumped. "I'm sorry." He

reached across the island and took my hand. "Do you want breakfast?"

"No."

Salvi came into the kitchen and smiled at me before addressing Romero.

"He's here," Salvi said.

"Send him in." Romero turned the kettle off as Salvi exited the kitchen.

"Who is here?" I asked, feeling a bit anxious. "Not the doctor again." I held up my hand. "I don't need another sedative. I don't want one."

"It's not Brett." He pointed to the entryway behind me. "You're going to like this guest."

I turned around, not quite believing who I saw standing in the doorway. "Sam."

"Hello, Lu."

I hopped off the stool and ran into his waiting arms. "What are you doing here?"

"I heard you were in the market for a new guard." He released me. "Will your old one work?"

"What?" I turned and looked at Romero. "Is this true?"

"Yes." Romero came and stood next to me. "I think you could use a familiar face around here."

"I can't believe this." The thought of being reunited with my longtime guard and friend was a dream come true. Sam and I had spent years together and when I married Romero, leaving Sam behind was difficult. "Wait." I thought for a moment. How was this even possible?

"What is it?" Romero asked.

"You won't betray us, right?" I hated to ask, but how could Romero trust him? "Look what my family made me do to Romero."

"You're a smart girl for asking, but you know I would

never do that to you." He glanced at Romero. "Your husband came to me and asked if I would protect you."

"After you let us go that night the Torrios had Luciana, I knew your loyalties were with my wife."

"I'm glad it worked out," Sam said. "There isn't anywhere else I'd rather be."

"How did it work out?" I didn't see my uncle letting a trusted guard quit so he could come work for a rival. "Why would they let you do this?"

"I haven't been working with the Torrios since that night Romero came for you." He shook his head. "I never appreciated the way they treated you, but I stood by and let it happen. That night I let the two of you go, I decided I had enough. I resigned and Mr. Torrio didn't give me any problems."

"That's surprising," I said. "He gives everyone a problem."

"After you married Mr. Bilotti they didn't have a whole lot of use for me. I mainly sat around monitoring visitors."

"You can call me Romero." He glanced at his watch. "I'm trusting you with the most precious person in my life."

"Are you sure you want to do this?" I asked. "The last person who came to work with us didn't have a happy ending."

"Luciana, I was sorry to hear about your friend," Sam said. "But, my position is different. I know the risks. My purpose is to keep you safe."

"Can you take me to see Stella's family?" I asked. "I want to pay my respects." I looked at Romero. "I'll be safe with Sam."

"No." Romero pressed his lips together, tightening his jaw. "I already told you no."

"Why?" I didn't understand. "We owe them a visit. She was killed in our home."

"That's why we can't go." He took a deep breath and slowly let it out. "Her husband made it very clear that he doesn't want me anywhere near his family. I have to respect his wishes. I may not like them, but it is what it is."

"Oh." I saw the hurt in his expression. Things like this didn't bother Romero. He was strong and didn't care what people thought about him. This bothered him. "I'm sorry. I didn't...I wasn't thinking about how her husband felt about the situation."

"It's okay." He kissed my cheek. "I have to meet Gio. We have some things to take care of today."

"Can't you take care of them here?" I wasn't ready for him to leave. "We don't know who murdered Stella. What if it isn't safe for you to leave?"

"I'll be fine." He smiled at me. "Promise me you'll eat something."

I nodded.

"Order from any restaurant in the city. Whatever you want can be delivered here. If they don't deliver, I'll make them." He winked. "Anything for you."

"I'll think about it." The thought of eating right now made my stomach churn.

"Sam, one of your duties is to make sure my wife eats something." Romero pointed at him. "I'll be home later."

"Wait." I chased after him. "Be careful."

"Always." He tilted my chin up and gently kissed me. "Don't worry."

That was easier said than done.

∼

I TRIED to focus on the laptop screen, but there was so much going on in my head. I thought getting back to my school work would help, but I was too sad to concentrate. All I could think about was Stella. When I thought about her, I tried to remember the happy times we had together. Every time I did, the image of her lying on the kitchen floor in a pool of blood in her purple Converse sneakers flooded my mind.

I leaned my head against the back of the sofa and closed my eyes, trying to think of a more positive memory. In the short time I had known her, I grew to love her.

"Keep the sauce on low." Stella washed her hands after rolling the meatballs. "And make sure you turn it."

"Turn it?"

"Yes, turn the sauce." She laughed. "My grandmother used to say that when she was making her sauce. Well, in our house we called it gravy,"

"Like brown gravy?"

"Some Italians call their sauce gravy. We always made gravy on Sundays. Anyway, when my grandmother said turn the sauce, she meant make sure I stirred it every so often so it wouldn't burn."

"Oh, so how long do I let it cook for?" I glanced at the recipe in Stella's family cookbook.

"Well, I like my sauce thick, so keep it on low for a few hours. After we fry the meatballs, we'll put them in and they'll absorb the flavors from the sauce."

"Did your grandma teach you how to cook?"

"Most of the Italian recipes. We always made fresh pasta to go with our sauce. You're good at making gnocchi now."

"Romero loves it."

"Next, I'll teach you how to make manicotti with a ricotta and spinach filling. It will pair perfect with these meatballs."

"Do your girls like to cook?"

"Not really." She shrugged. *"They like eating what I cook."*

"Maybe when they're out of school they will appreciate cooking more."

"I'm happy you're learning from me." She set a large pan on the stove and filled it with oil. *"I like knowing someone will carry on my traditions when I'm gone."*

"Where are you going?" I took the wooden spoon and stirred the sauce.

"Nowhere if I can help it." She smiled. *"That was something my grandmother used to say too. You're going to miss me when I'm gone, she'd say."* She placed the raw meatballs into the pan. *"She was right."*

"I'm so glad you came into my life."

"The feeling is mutual."

"I'd like to meet your girls." I wanted to see her interact with her children, but mostly I wanted to tell them what an amazing woman they had in their lives. They were so lucky to have a mom like her.

"I'd like that too." She fried the meatballs. *"We'll set up a lunch date. I think it might be nice for you to meet some people close to your age."*

"Instead of hanging out with those bodyguards all day?"

"They're easy on the eyes, aren't they?" She giggled.

"Very much." I blushed. *"But don't tell Romero I said that. He would fire all of them."*

"It's our secret."

A commotion in the hall outside the front door drew me out of the memory.

"Let's get him inside," Gio said. "The doctor is on his way."

I hurried off the couch and to the door as it swung open.

His Broken Queen 59

Gio quickly came in, widening the door to let those behind him in.

"Gio." When he turned to face me, the expression on his face startled me.

"Lu." His light blue dress shirt was stained with red blotches on it and his hands were covered in blood.

"Whose blood is that?" I didn't have to ask because instinct had already answered the question.

Gio came to stand with me as Joey and Salvi held Romero up and guided him into the room.

"Oh, no!" I screamed. "No!"

CHAPTER 8

Romero

I met Gio at the club to handle a few things. I didn't like running our illegitimate business from Cantinos, but because the house was still a crime scene, and I didn't want to conduct these particular dealings with Lu at the penthouse, this location was our only choice.

"Thanks again for letting us stay at the penthouse." I sat behind the desk in the back office. "As soon as the cops are done with their useless investigation we should be out of your way."

"Stay as long as you need to."

"I'm sure we're interfering in your sex life." I smirked. "After a few more nights you'll be throwing us out of there."

"My sex life wasn't that great before you came to stay with me." He frowned. "You keep me so busy, I don't have time for it."

"Sorry to hear that."

"I sat with Lu last night."

"How did she seem?"

"She's really sad." He leaned against the desk. "It's not fair for one woman to know so much pain."

"Hooking up with me didn't help matters."

"She would be the first one to tell you, you're the best thing that's ever happened to her."

"It's the other way around. Besides, she might not feel like that anymore." I was the one who brought Stella into our home to help with Lu's isolation. "An innocent woman is dead because of me. One who she cared for very much."

"You can keep saying that, but it's not your fault. We have to find the fuckers who did this and show them our style of retaliation."

"I will kill the person responsible for this."

Salvi knocked on the door before opening it.

"Antonio Torrio is here to see you," he said. "He says you're expecting him."

"Maybe we'll get some answers." I stood from the desk and buttoned my suit jacket. "Send him in."

Antonio told his guard to wait by the door before entering the office and closing the door. He nodded at Gio before acknowledging me. I thought it was odd he was alone.

"Where is Vincent?" I didn't expect Rocco to take this meeting with him, but I wouldn't have thought he would come without one of his other sons.

"He's busy," he said. "Do I need him here?"

"No."

"I don't appreciate being summoned," he said. "But because you are my niece's husband, I'll make an exception."

"I don't appreciate having my house ambushed and having an innocent friend murdered in said house." I gripped the edge of my desk. "And don't use my wife as an excuse for anything."

"I only meant that I'm here because I know Luciana was close to Stella." He shook his head. "How is my niece?"

"How do you think she is?" I snapped. "She's devastated, but it isn't like you care."

"I'm going to ignore your tone, and the fact that you asking me to come here today insinuates that you think I'm responsible for such a hideous act." He scowled. "It's disgraceful and makes all of us look bad that someone would be so animalistic as to kill a woman who had nothing to do with our business."

"Stella wasn't supposed to be there, so if it was a botched hit on me, she surprised them and paid with her life."

"Frankie LaVanza's son was gunned down in Brooklyn an hour ago," he said. "That was not a botched hit."

"What?" Gio took out his phone and did a search. "What the hell?" He nodded at me with confirmation.

"If you remember," Antonio continued, "two of LaVanza's top soldiers were taken out a few months ago with no explanation. His family is being targeted. Your house was targeted. The other families are laying low. Dante Marchelli has increased security and won't let any of his family leave the compound."

"Santino is in Brazil," I said.

"Dante is trying to get him home as soon as possible." Antonio took a seat across from my desk. "I know his family stands with you, so I figured you would want to know."

"We need to call Dominick Marchelli and tell him we can help with whatever they need to get Santino home," I said to Gio.

"I'll do it after this meeting," Gio said.

"What's going on?" I asked Antonio.

"These occurrences are not coming from any of the lead families," Antonio said. "We've all been paralyzed these past few months because of the Feds and the cartel."

"Everything was fine before you came after me." I gritted my teeth. "Was it worth setting in motion what you have?"

"Was it worth you marrying my niece and exposing my son's paternity?" Antonio slammed his fist on the arm of the chair. "You seem to have made out pretty good."

"Those things happened because of you, but I will never regret finding Luciana and getting her away from you and your crazy wife." I controlled the urge to pull out my gun and shoot him in the head. "As for Rocco, that was not my doing. If you hadn't taken Lu from me, none of that mess would have been exposed that night. You only have yourself to blame."

"That's a fair point." He sighed. "That is a problem for another day. We have bigger concerns. I'll admit, I came after you because when you came back to New York, I thought you would eventually want to take your rightful place as your father's heir. You were a threat to all of us."

"I never wanted a seat at the table." I pointed at him. "I was fine with working peacefully with the families. I would move my products through your harbors and you all would get your fair share. I never crossed anyone. I never took more than I was owed."

"I didn't trust you," he said.

"Obviously," Gio said. "You went through great lengths to stop us."

"I miscalculated." He stared at me. "I'd heard things about you. I had good reasons to believe you were in the city to take what was mine."

"Giancarlo?" I waved my hand in the air. "He was a traitor playing both sides, but you couldn't figure that out."

"Which is why he's nowhere to be found?" Antonio arched his brow.

"I don't know where he is, but he won't show his face in front of me again." I made sure of that. "You acted on assumptions and someone else's lies. That doesn't make for a very smart businessman much less the top Don on the East coast. You sacrificed your niece, knowing if I found out I could kill her."

"You did find out and you didn't kill her,." He smirked. "I'd say it worked out rather well for you."

"Except for the part where I can't move my product in the states." I balled my fist by my side. "If you left me alone we'd all be a little richer right now and maybe none of us would be worried about being taken out."

"That's in the past," he said. "None of us are safe until we figure out who is targeting us. We're going to have to work together to figure this out."

"Are you kidding me?" I laughed at the absurdity. "What? Do you want to make an alliance? I've been there and done that. No fucking way."

"Romero, don't be like your father." He stood. "Now is not the time to let your pride get in the way."

"I'll accept that you aren't responsible for Stella's death, but that's all the courtesy I'll extend to you. I can protect my own. Stay out of my way."

"I thought you'd say that, so I'm going to give you something as a show of faith."

"What?" I rolled my eyes. "You don't have anything I need."

"Don't be so sure."

"What do you have for us?" Gio asked.

"I spoke with Senator Collins today. He owes me a rather large favor, one that I've been waiting to cash in on. This one will benefit all of us and give us the time to eliminate whoever is coming after the New York mafia. This will be of particular interest to you."

"I'm listening."

"As of this afternoon, Agent Carson Morgan is being transferred to the California bureau. He will no longer be assigned to any cases involving organized crime."

Impressive.

"Of course, another agent will take over and probably be just as much if not more of a nuisance, but that won't be for a few weeks. We can do what needs to be done. Don't squander this opportunity."

He opened the door and then looked over his shoulder at me. "Watch your back, and that's not a threat. It's a genuine sentiment." He shut the door behind him.

"What the fuck was that?" Gio asked. "Now he wants to work with us?"

"He knows something big is brewing and he needs us on his side." I sat on the edge of the desk. "Where are we with those DNA results?"

"I went with Rocco this morning and submitted to the test. I had our guy at the lab put a rush on it."

"I believe Antonio knows the truth about Rocco's paternity, but Kristina can't be trusted. For all we know, Antonio could be his father if she was sleeping with both of them at the same time."

"Why do you think Dad wouldn't pursue that? He was so territorial. If there was a possibility that he had another son, wouldn't he have insisted on a paternity test?"

"Who knows?" I rubbed my temples, trying to ward off the impending headache. "I've been away from Luciana long enough. I need to get back and check on her."

"I can leave with you," he said. "Let me text the guys and

have them bring the car around the back. The less we're seen here today, the better."

"Do you want to go on lockdown like the Marchellis?"

"Someone is coming for the families." Gio sent the text and shoved his phone in his pocket. "There's no reason not to take precautions."

"I agree."

We walked out of the office and down the back stairs to the doors that led to the alley way.

"The penthouse is the best bet for now." When Gio opened the doors, the sunlight poured in, making it difficult to see the street. "We can control who comes in and out. No one can get through the building security without us okaying it."

"It's probably better for now." I put my sunglasses on. "Lu's not ready to go back to our house anyway." I wasn't sure when or if she would ever be ready to go back home.

Once we stepped outside, the sound of screeching tires caught my attention. I turned my head just as Joey pulled the SUV up in front of us. The car with the loud tires stopped in the cross street and rolled down the tinted windows.

"Fuck!" Gio shouted.

I looked back at him as Salvi drew his gun amidst the booming sound of gun fire. I reached for my gun and took aim. When I raised my arm to fire, an excruciating pain ripped through me. Gio opened the car door and shoved me inside.

He helped me up from the floor of the car as Salvi got in the back with us and slammed the door.

"Drive!" Salvi shouted at Joey. "Fucking run them over if you have to."

The bullets bounced off the windows as Joey floored it,

but I couldn't focus on what was happening because something wasn't right. Pain radiated through my left shoulder. I glanced down at my suit jacket because it felt wet, but the material was too dark for me to see anything. When I pressed my hand against the jacket, blood transferred onto my palm.

"Shit."

"What?" Gio asked.

"I think I..." I unbuttoned my jacket as the blood seeped through my shirt.

"Were you hit?" Gio pushed my jacket over my shoulder. "Christ, Romero."

I squeezed my eyes shut as the sweat dripped down my face.

"Get me to Luciana right now." I dropped my arm down, letting my gun fall to the floor. "I have to make sure she's okay."

"Romero!" Gio called my name, but I didn't respond. "Take him to the penthouse."

CHAPTER 9

Luciana

The guys helped Romero into the penthouse as Gio ushered me out of the way.

"Put him on the dining room table." Gio pointed. "Jag, go grab sheets and towels from the upstairs hall closet."

Joey and Salvi took Romero to the table while Jag ran up the steps.

"What happened?" I ran to Romero. "Oh." I put my hand over my mouth when I saw his bloodstained shirt. "Romero." I took his frigid hand in mine, noting how pale he looked.

"I'm okay, butterfly." His words were strained. "I'll be fine."

"Why didn't you call an ambulance or bring him to the hospital?" I asked. "Why is he here?"

"It's better this way." Gio took a pillow from the sofa and propped Romero's head. "Brett will be here in a few minutes. He can take the bullet out."

"What?" I kissed Romero's forehead. "You have to go to the hospital. You can't take a bullet out here."

"No, Lu." Romero closed his eyes. "I can't take this war inside a hospital. There can't be any record of this."

"Why? Someone shot you." When I said those words, my stomach hurt. Someone shot Stella too, and now…

"If I go to the hospital, they will call the police. I don't need that aggravation. I'll get my own justice."

"Here." Gio lifted the back of Romero's head and pressed a bottle of vodka to his lips. "Drink that."

Romero gulped the alcohol, never letting go of my hand.

Jag unbuttoned Romero's shirt, and wiped the blood from his shoulder. When Romero winced, Gio gave him more to drink.

"Try to relax," Gio said. "This will be over soon. Brett will give you something to take the edge off."

How were they all so calm? My husband was lying on the dining room table with a bullet lodged in his shoulder, bleeding out, but no one seemed to be that bothered by it.

"You're shaking." Romero looked at me.

"I'm sorry."

"Don't apologize." He tugged on my arm because he wanted me closer. "Come here."

I leaned down, close to his face, trying to hold back the tears, but I couldn't stop them.

"Baby, I'll be fine. I promise." He smiled. "This is nothing."

"You're in pain." I stroked his cheek. "What can I do for you?"

"Just be here." He brushed his lips across mine. "You're all I need."

"I need you," I whispered. "You can't go around getting shot."

"They're not going to get a second chance at me, baby. I promise." He closed his eyes and took a deep breath. "Fuck."

"Can't we give him something for the pain?" I asked.

"Brett's on his way up," Gio said. "He'll take care of him."

How was he going to take care of him? This wasn't a hospital. Romero needed a sanitary space with pain medicine and sterile equipment.

"I think we should go to the hospital." I pressed my lips to Romero's. "It'll be safer for you. Please."

"I'm okay, baby girl." He rested his palm against my cheek. "Just don't leave me, okay?"

"I would never."

"What do we have?" Brett came into the room with his black bag and glanced at Romero's shoulder. "It doesn't look too bad."

"The bullet didn't go through," Gio said. "Do you think you can remove it?"

When my knees buckled and I trembled a little harder, Romero smiled at me, trying to comfort me. It wasn't working, and I should be the one comforting him.

"He needs to go to the hospital." I said as Brett went to the kitchen and washed his hands. Shouldn't a doctor know that?

All the guys gathered around the table. This was Romero's operating room team? My stomach churned and I thought I might be sick, but I couldn't leave his side.

"Luciana." Brett came back into the room and put on a pair of gloves. "If Romero could go to the hospital, I wouldn't be here. I promise I've done this before. I won't let anything happen to him."

"I will kill you myself if something happens to my brother." Gio warned him. "Get moving so he can settle down and rest."

"Everyone back up and let me work," Brett said. "I don't need a team."

"Let's stop fucking around and get this done." Romero gritted his teeth when Brett examined his shoulder.

"Gio help me sit him up." Brett slid his arm under Romero's back as Gio assisted getting Romero into a seated position.

Romero gripped my hand as he scooted into a seated position. His damp hair fell onto his forehead as the sweat trickled down his face. His jaw tightened when Brett injected him with something I assumed was for the pain.

"Let's cut this shirt off him." Brett handed Joey a pair of scissors. "Then I can get to work."

"Lu, you need to switch places with Gio." Romero's voice was weak.

"What? No, I want to be close to you."

"Don't argue with me." He took a breath as Joey cut the shirt off him. "I don't want to break your hand."

"I don't...what do you mean?" I asked.

"Beauty." Gio placed his hand on the small of my back. "He's going to have to squeeze really hard when that bullet comes out. He won't break my hand, and if he does, he will forgive himself a lot easier than if he breaks yours."

"I might break yours, Gio." Romero jumped when Brett did something to his wound. "Just for a few minutes, Lu."

I reluctantly let go of his hand. I wanted to make this easier for him, but I wanted to be as close to him as possible.

"Stay where I can see you, baby."

I stood next to Gio as he took Romero's hand. I wiped the tears away from my cheeks as the doctor did his thing.

"Don't cry," Romero said. "I can handle this."

I didn't watch what Brett was doing because I wanted to stay focused on my husband. When all the color drained from his face, I knew he was in a tremendous amount of pain, but he pressed his lips together and gripped his brother's hand as Brett worked to dig out the bullet. I placed my hand on his thigh so he could feel me.

He yelled out his favorite four-letter word a few times, and they had to stop the procedure so Romero could catch his breath and drink some more vodka.

Once the bullet was out, they laid him on his side so Brett could clean him up and stitch the opening. Romero's eyes became heavy, but he tried to keep them open.

"Looks like the meds are finally kicking in," Gio said.

"He should be groggy for a while, but that will help him heal." Brett continued to work. "It was a clean entry. He's going to be sore and he'll have to wear a sling for a few days, which he'll hate, but I want to keep that shoulder immobile. The less he uses it, the better for now."

"He's going to be okay?" When I took Romero's hand, he relaxed and closed his eyes. "What do we need to do for him?"

"Let him rest. Make sure he drinks fluids, preferably not vodka. I'm going to prescribe antibiotics and pain medicine. There is a risk of infection, but the medication should help."

Brett gave more instructions on how to care for him, but the only thing I could concentrate on was Romero. Someone tried to kill him today. They didn't succeed, but that wouldn't stop them from trying again. I could lose him next time. How was I supposed to deal with that?

"Lu." Gio put his hand on my shoulder. "We're going to move him upstairs now. I can sit with him until you get yourself situated."

"I can stay with him." I wiped my eyes. "I want to stay with him."

"I think you might need a few minutes to compose yourself. This is upsetting. When I saw that he was hit, I thought..." Gio shook his head. "I could sit with him for a bit while you shower or do whatever you need to do, and you can have the night shift."

"I'm okay, but I'll grab some water and get changed." I could see the relief on Gio's face now that Romero was resting, but it must have been difficult to see his brother get shot. "You go upstairs with him." I wanted to give him a few minutes with Romero. "I'll be up soon."

"Thanks." He kissed my cheek. "He's going to be fine. He knows how much we need him."

I nodded as Joey and Salvi carried Romero up the stairs. Once they were out of sight, I went to the kitchen, and splashed some water on my face. The shock of seeing Stella shot in our house still hadn't worn off. I didn't know if it ever would. Now, I had to deal with the fact that someone wanted to kill Romero. It was always a possibility, but it was something I tried not to think about.

I put my hand over my mouth and tried to conceal the sobs that insisted on escaping from some place deep inside my chest. I shook uncontrollably as I slid down the wall, sat on the floor, and pulled my knees to my chest. How much more could I take?

I took some time to cry. I only needed a few minutes to get this out. Then I would be strong for Romero. He needed me now, and I would be there for him the way he was always there for me.

My heart ached when I thought about how easily this could have gone the other way. I could have lost him today. I could be mourning him the way I was Stella.

"Hey." Jag came into the kitchen, and then sat down on the floor next to me. "He's going to be alright."

"I know." I ran my hands over my face. "I just needed a minute."

"I understand." He started to get up. "I'll leave you alone."

"No." I reached for him. "Stay."

"Okay."

"It's been a rough few days."

"I'm really sorry about Stella." When he paused, I could see his expression change. "She was very nice to me, especially after, well, you know."

"After Romero lost his shit on you?"

He shook his head because he didn't think I knew about the beating he took the day Vincent kidnapped me.

"I saw your face and you had trouble walking for a few days after what happened with me and Vincent. Romero did that to you." My husband could be brutal when the situation called for it. "I'm sorry about that."

"You have nothing to be sorry for."

"It was my fault."

"No, it wasn't. I should never have let you go into that restaurant alone. Romero was right to take his anger out on me. I had the most important job on the team, and I screwed up."

"I thought I was meeting Sandro."

"But I need to learn how to anticipate that kind of thing. That's why I can't be your guard anymore. I can't risk your safety, and not just because Romero would kill me if something happened to you, but because I would never forgive myself. I'm sorry I let Vincent take you that day."

"Despite what my husband thinks, I am my own person, and I got out of that car and walked into the restaurant because I wanted to. I should have respected that you had a job to do and I should have waited for you to park the car. I'm very sorry that you took the brunt of Romero's anger."

"It's okay."

"For what it's worth, I do miss you as my guard. I miss our talks, and the time we used to spend together."

"Me too." He smiled. "Sam will take good care of you."

"You're staying on with us, right?"

"As long as Romero and Gio will have me, I'd like to stay."

"I'm glad to hear that." I stood from the floor, wishing I could reassure him, but I had no control over what Romero did when it came to his business. "I better go check on him."

He nodded as he got up.

"Thanks for staying with me."

"Anytime."

I took my time heading to the bedroom. I had to take care of Romero tonight. He needed me, and I wanted to be there for him. I loved him more than I hated his world, but it was getting harder to understand why he chose this life.

∽

A FEW HOURS LATER, I set my book down on the nightstand and crawled into bed next to Romero. He had been sleeping, but the pain meds were wearing off. He had become increasingly restless over the last thirty minutes.

As I cuddled against him, the heat from his body transferred to my skin. I sat up and put my palm to his forehead.

"You're burning up." I jumped out of bed and went to the bathroom to get a cool washcloth.

When I came back, he was reaching for my side of the bed.

"Luciana," his gruff voice called for me.

"I'm here." I got into bed, and then pressed the cloth to his head.

I took the bottle of water from the nightstand, removing the cap before I propped his head. "Take a sip of this." I poured a small amount into his mouth.

He swallowed, and then held up his hand and shook his head.

"You have to stay hydrated." I caressed his cheek. "I think you have a fever."

"I'm sorry."

"For what?"

"Everything." His eyes were still closed, and I wasn't sure if he was even awake. "I hurt you."

"No, you didn't." I gently kissed his lips. "Try and relax."

"I was mean to you when we met." He ripped the washcloth from his head. "I married you even though I knew you didn't want to marry me."

"I want to be married to you." I took the cloth from him and put it on his head. "I love you."

He was quiet for a few minutes, and I thought maybe he had settled down.

"I don't deserve you," he mumbled. "But I can't let you go."

"I'm not going anywhere." I curled into his side. "I want to take care of you the way you take care of me."

"I'm sorry, Lu." His breaths were labored. "I'm sorry about Stella. I'm sorry about your parents. My life has caused you nothing but misery."

"That's not true." He wouldn't remember this conversation in the morning, but maybe he would tire himself out enough to fall asleep. "I don't blame you for anything."

"My father killed your parents."

"That wasn't your fault."

"I'm so sorry."

I didn't need him to apologize, but maybe he needed to purge himself of his guilt to heal. He was such a tortured soul. I wanted more than anything for him to leave this life behind, and start over. It wasn't a practical dream, but it was my dream.

I rested my head on his chest, and listened to his breathing. He appeared calmer. He was still running a fever, but I hoped once the antibiotics kicked in he would feel better.

"I love you," he whispered. "Don't leave me."

"Not ever."

CHAPTER 10

Romero

"Gio!" I shouted from the study in the penthouse.

I had been stuck here for over two days. My shoulder hurt and I wanted this damn sling off, but every time I tried Gio or Luciana insisted I needed it.

"Gio!" My patience couldn't take much more. "Where are you?"

"I'm coming." My brother entered the study, mumbling something in Italian. "What is it?" He looked me over. "Leave that on." He pointed to the sling. "I mean it."

"I fucking hate it."

"Too bad. You need it." He shut the door. "You have to relax. No one wants to be around you. They're all going to quit."

"Relax?" I threw my hand in the air. "How can I relax? Someone took a shot at us."

"That will be one of the last things they do."

"We have to fucking catch them first." I clenched my fist,

wishing the pain meds could take this ache away. "I can't be cooped up here much longer."

"We don't have a choice." He shook his head. "We have to figure out what is going on and who is responsible. I can't get any information on the street. People are scared. That's not usual."

"Someone will slip up and say what they know, and when they do, I'm not holding back. They started this war, but I'll finish it."

"I spoke with the Malatesta family."

The Malatestas were a prominent family in Italy. They ran many of the products in and out of their country. If anyone wanted anything moved, they had to go through them. When our father died, and Gio and I relocated to Italy, they took us under their wing, and helped us get established.

"How did that go?"

"Janero is disappointed with us. He doesn't trust Antonio."

"I should have sought his advice when Antonio came to me with the alliance, but I trusted Giancarlo."

"He said you were stupid."

"We hit a rough patch. If we can get back in with the cartel, we'll be up and running again."

"He doesn't think we'll be able to do that on our own."

"He's probably right." I hated having to call in favors, but I was boxed into a corner and needed to get out. "What do you think?"

"We need to hear him out. It might end up costing us, but right now we're not doing so well. Our options are limited."

"A trip might be necessary."

"It might not be a bad idea. No one here will dare come after us on Malatesta territory. It could buy us some time."

"What is that?" I pointed to the envelope he held. "Is it a potential problem?"

The way my week was going, why not add to it?

"I hope not." He stared down at the envelope. "It's the DNA results."

"Did you open it?" I wanted a rush on the results, but I wasn't sure if I was ready for the answer.

"Rocco's on his way up." He held up the results. "I figured we should wait for him."

"It's going to be a hell of a lot less complicated if he's a Torrio." I took a seat at the desk. "Vincent and Antonio aren't going to like the alternative."

"What about us? What does it mean if he is a Bilotti?"

"We'll cross that bridge when we come to it, but he can't be loyal to both families. He may be able to co-exist between us, but in the end, he'll have to make a decision. It will come down to who he chooses."

"I don't envy him."

"This is just another way Dad screwed us." I tapped my fingers on the desk. "There isn't anything we can do about it now. It is what it is."

"You've been saying that a lot."

"We've been dealing with a lot of shit."

The knock at the door halted Gio's response.

"We're about to find out what it is." Gio opened the door. "Rocco, come in."

"How are you?" Rocco asked.

"I survived." I leaned back in my chair. "I'll feel better when I retaliate."

He nodded.

"I'm guessing you're here because of this?" Gio held up the results.

"You got them too?"

"I didn't open them yet," Gio said. "I wanted to wait for you."

"I didn't either." Rocco took out an envelope from his inside pocket. "I thought I should do it in front of you both, so there were no doubts."

"Let's get it over with," I said.

Gio shot me a displeased look, but I didn't have any more fucks to give this morning.

Rocco opened his envelope, and then took his time reading the results. Gio and I watched as he soaked in the information. For a man with an Ivy League education, it took him long enough to process what he read. Maybe he just didn't want to accept it.

"What does it say?" Gio asked.

"We're a match." He placed the results back in the envelope, and shoved them in his pocket.

"It's really not a shock, right?" Gio looked at me. "It's what we suspected."

"Seeing it in black and white makes it real, you know?" Rocco took a breath. "When I told my mother I was getting the test, she left to visit some cousins in France. No one has any idea when she's coming back."

Fucking bitch.

"I guess she already knew what these results would be," Rocco said.

"I don't know what to say." Gio approached him. "I mean, should I shake your hand, hug you?"

"Not sure."

"Welcome to the family, man." Gio patted his back.

"Thanks." Rocco shrugged. "This is a lot to process."

"You're awfully quiet." Gio motioned toward me. "This is big news."

What does he want me to say?

"It's a lot for all of us," Rocco said. "I'll leave you two alone so you can discuss it."

"You don't have anything to say to him?" Gio asked. "This isn't his fault."

"Oh, I have plenty to say, but I'm not sure our *brother* wants to hear it." I stood from the desk, and came around to where Gio and Rocco were. I was still the head of this family, and I would speak my mind.

"Ignore him." Gio went to the shelves in the corner of the room and took out the decanter filled with the expensive vodka. "He's in a bad mood because he got shot and he has to wear that sling."

"We still don't know who did that." I looked at Rocco. "Any ideas?"

"If you're asking if I had anything to do with it, I didn't."

"Maybe not you, but what about the rest of your family?" There had been chaos among the leading families for weeks, so the feud between us and the Torrios had been shelved, but I hadn't forgotten what they had done. "That piece of paper doesn't mean I'm going to automatically trust you."

"I wouldn't expect you to." Rocco took a glass from Gio. "I don't trust you either."

"There's bad blood between our families. I can't easily forget that bullshit alliance, even if I did benefit from it."

Gio set my glass of vodka on the desk.

"Which brings me to my next point," I said. "You've treated my wife like she didn't matter her whole life."

"I've always cared for Lu," Rocco defended.

"You were young when she came to live with you, and

you were influenced by the way your parents treated her, but you did know that Vincent planned to drug her and take her away from me. Am I supposed to forget that?"

"I didn't know he was going to drug her," he said. "But I agree, we didn't treat her right. I didn't want her to marry you, but now I know that was the best thing for her. That shit alliance was a stupid plan, but it led Lu to you, so I won't regret my part in it."

"I don't trust easily, but I can't deny that Bilotti blood runs through your veins. I don't know what you're going to do with that, but you have been there for us these last few days. You took care of Morgan, and you helped with the police search the other night."

"I did what I could." He took a sip of his drink. "My father..." He cleared his throat. "Antonio told me Agent Morgan is being transferred. His replacement is going to be more appropriate when it comes to our business. The Senator confirmed that yesterday."

"I hope so." I raised my glass. "This is going to be an adjustment for all of us."

Gio and Rocco raised their glasses.

"I want to get to know the two of you," Rocco said. "I want to know where I come from, but I can't forget who I've been all these years. I can't walk away from my family."

"No one is asking you to," Gio said.

"It doesn't matter what those results proved." I finished my drink. "Our father was no better than Antonio, but at least Antonio managed to live, and got you an education. Our father left us to the streets. Sure, we had money, and a lot of it, but we were trained for this life at an early age. That's all we know."

"That's all I know," Rocco said. "And now, after thirty years of believing I was a Torrio, I find out my whole life was a lie. I don't know where I belong, but I have to figure it out."

"You will." Gio poured another round. "Right now, we all have to be on guard. We have to find the bastard who is targeting us."

"Has there been any progress with finding out who was responsible for the attack on your home?" Rocco asked. "Now that Morgan is gone, the investigation will slow down."

"That's what we want." I downed my vodka. "I don't need their interference."

"Would it be okay if I had a look at the security footage from that night?" Rocco finished his drink. "Maybe if I look at it with a fresh set of eyes, I might see something you missed."

"That's a good idea," Gio said. "I'll send it to you."

I sat down at the desk, and scrolled through my phone as Gio and Rocco made small talk. Gio was a good judge of character, but he was more trusting than I was. As Rocco talked, I noted his mannerisms. They were more familiar than I had realized. Studying his strong profile, I saw the resemblance that I hadn't found before. His dark hair and olive colored skin could have easily been the result of Torrio DNA. We were all Italian, and had some of the same genetic traits, but now that I really looked at him, the truth couldn't be concealed any longer. I saw my father's eyes, Gio's jawline, and my tall, muscular frame.

When Rocco took a seat by the window, his posture was straight and his speech so articulate. He commanded respect. I always pegged him as being the smartest Torrio, and now I know why. He was a Bilotti the whole time.

"What do you think?" Gio's voice pulled me from my thoughts.

"About?" I looked at him.

"Weren't you listening?" Gio waved his hand to dismiss me. "Never mind."

"I should get going." Rocco headed toward the door. "I need to tell Vincent and Sandro about these results."

"Rocco." I stopped him before he could leave. "You're still the same person you were this morning."

"But you have two more brothers," Gio said. "If you want them."

"I appreciate it."

When he opened the door, Luciana stood on the other side with her hand up as if she was about to knock.

"Oh." She tucked her hair behind her ear. "I didn't realize you were here."

"I was just leaving." Rocco smiled. "You look lovely."

"I...ah." Lu looked at me from the doorway as she fidgeted with the hem of her dress.

She wore a simple black dress, light makeup dusted her face, and her hair was blown out in a sleek, long style. This was the first time since Stella's death that she appeared like herself. Her stunning beauty took my breath away, and I might have told her if I wasn't seeing red.

Did she honestly believe I would approve of this?

"Going somewhere?" I came around and joined them at the door, and true to her character, she backed away from me.

"I, well, I'm going to Stella's funeral."

"The fuck you are."

CHAPTER 11

Luciana

This was a hard sell, but I wouldn't let Romero talk me out of it. I needed to do this.

"I have to go," I said. "I'm not asking."

"Fuck," Gio mumbled under his breath.

"Well, I'm *telling* you that you can't go." Romero stared me down. "We are not welcome there, and we're going to respect the family's wishes. We've caused them enough heartache."

"You're not welcome there." I didn't want to point that out, but I had to go to Stella's funeral. Surely, the family didn't blame me for what had happened.

"They don't want anyone from this family there," he shouted. "Can you blame them?"

"Romero, please." My eyes filled with tears, but I tried to hold them back. "I can't live the rest of my life without this closure. I owe it to Stella to be there."

"Lu." He took my hand, trying to soften his demeanor. "I understand. I do, but this isn't about you. It's about Stella's family and what they want right now."

"I won't upset them." The tears streamed down my cheeks. "I asked Sam to take me, but he said he can't unless you tell him he can. Please tell him he can."

"Don't cry." He wiped my face with his fingers. "It's not safe. I can't go with you. I can't let you go alone."

"I'll be fine."

"No." He let go of my hand. "That's the end of this discussion. I have work to do."

"I'm going to that funeral, so if you won't give Sam permission to take me, I'll call a ride share."

"Are you out of your fucking mind?" When he yelled, I backed away, bumping into Rocco. "Do you want to get shot next?"

"Lu." Gio tried to guide me out of the study. "This really isn't a good time."

"If I wait for a good time, I'll miss the funeral." I moved closer to Romero. "You know I have to do this."

"And you know I have to keep you safe." He tucked my hair behind my ear. "I'm sorry."

"What if I went with her?" Rocco offered. "I have two guys downstairs and Sam could go with us. I wouldn't leave her side."

"Please." I begged Romero.

"Where's the funeral?" Rocco asked.

"Rappaselli's," Gio said.

"I know the funeral director." Rocco took out his phone. "I'll call him and tell him Lu has to come through the back. There's less of a chance of anyone seeing her on the street."

"It could work," Gio said. "If she's in and out, and heavily guarded, she'll be safe."

"Please, Romero." I took his hand. "I won't stay long. I just want to pay my respects. I have to go for Stella."

"I can make the call," Rocco said. "It's not a problem."

Romero stared at me for a moment before nodding to Rocco.

"Thank you!" When I hugged him, he held me tight, lingering for a while. "I'm going to be okay."

"I'll make sure her security is ready to go." Gio left the study.

"I'll call the funeral home," Rocco said. "Lu, I'll see you in a few minutes."

"Thanks." I wiped my face as they left the room.

"Rocco is right." Romero released me. "You do look lovely."

"I wish I was going anywhere but there."

"I still think it's a mistake." He leaned against the desk. "But, you're determined, so what can I do?"

"I have to do this."

"I don't like to be challenged," he said. "Especially not in front of my brothers."

"Your...wait? Rocco is your brother?" I had a suspicion that would be the case, but I wasn't sure Romero was going to accept it. "You know for sure?"

"The results were confirmed this morning." He winced when he maneuvered his shoulder inside the sling. "That's why he's here. Luckily, for you, he was or you wouldn't be going to the funeral."

"You're upset."

"You think?" He pushed off the desk and paced the room. "I'm losing control and I don't fucking like it," he yelled. "A family friend was murdered in my home, someone took a shot at me and my men, my wife is defiant, and oh, yeah, I have a long lost brother from a rival family. I'd say I'm upset."

I jumped when he slammed his fist against the wall.

"I'm sorry." I came behind him and wrapped my arms around his waist.

"For being defiant?"

"No." I kissed the side of his neck. "But for all the other stuff."

"Lu." He turned in my arms. "I'm trying to protect you."

"You heard Rocco." I rested my head on his uninjured shoulder. "No one is going to come after me at the funeral. I'm not even supposed to be there."

"That's not what I'm trying to protect you from." He took my upper arm in his hand. "You've been through enough this week. You don't need any more stress."

"I'm stronger than you think." I kissed his cheek. "I'll be fine."

"Don't think we're not going to address this stunt you pulled this morning." He tightened his jaw. "You're lucky I didn't lock you in a room."

"Would you have locked yourself in there with me?"

"If that was what it took."

"You know I still want to run away with you. We could leave everything behind and go on an adventure."

I dreamed that the two of us could leave everything behind and start over. No violence, no guards, no guns.

"We still haven't gone on a honeymoon." I bit my lip. "Maybe you need a vacation."

"I need you." He cupped my chin between his fingers. "Nothing else matters."

Gio tapped on the door.

"What?" Romero growled.

"The car is downstairs," Gio said. "Joey will drive. Sam and Rocco will ride with Lu."

"Rocco's men?"

"They'll be in the car behind them. Lu will go in through the back, pay her respects, and leave." Gio widened the door. "You should go now before the visitation gets too crowded."

"Send Jag in the car with Rocco's men," Romero said. "Have Rocco accompany Lu into the funeral home. We can't make a display of all these guards walking in, but make sure Sam is right outside the funeral home."

"I'll take care of it," Gio said. "Come on, Lu."

"Thank you," I whispered.

"In and out, Luciana. I want you back here as soon as possible." He grabbed me by the waist, and engulfed me in a strong hold with his good arm, and lowered his lips to mine. His possessive kiss left me breathless. "Go." He let go of me, and pointed to the door.

I dropped my gaze to the floor, and left the room without looking into his eyes. I didn't want to meet the disapproval in them. I had to get through this next hour. It was going to be one of the toughest, most grueling situations of my life, and I had to do it without Romero by my side.

∼

As we pulled into the alleyway behind the funeral home, the ache in my stomach turned into a vicious churning. When Joey got out and opened the passenger side door, I froze.

"Lu?" Rocco touched my arm. "Are you ready?"

I shook my head.

"Give us a minute," Rocco said to Joey.

"Romero said in and out, remember?" Joey glanced at his watch.

"Just wait by the door." Rocco pointed. "We'll be right there."

Joey did what Rocco asked as I tried to settle my stomach with some deep breaths.

"What's going on, Lu?"

"What if Romero is right? What if I shouldn't be here?"

"You were pretty certain you should be here when you stood up to your husband and told him you were going. That's why I stepped in to help you." He gazed out the front window of the car. "What changed?"

"Now that we're here, I guess I'm nervous." I wanted to be brave, and do the right thing. "I really miss her."

"Then you're doing the right thing." He motioned toward the funeral home. "If you don't go in, you'll regret it. I can't say it will be easy to face Stella's kids, but if you don't find the closure you're searching for today, you might not ever. I don't want that for you."

"Don't you get tired of this life?" I asked. "You're an educated man. You have so many opportunities and privileges."

"I have those things because of this life."

"I have Romero because of this life, but it doesn't mean I don't hope that one day he finds a way out. He's smart and knows how to run a business. Look what he's done with the club. Maybe he'll realize that's enough. I'm enough."

"His love for you has nothing to do with what he chooses to do for a living. He was in this world long before he met you, and to be honest, he's going to be in it for years to come." He patted the top of my hand. "You might not want to hear that, but it's the way it is for men like us. We don't have the luxury to choose."

"I can still dream."

"You shouldn't give up your dreams." He winked. "But if you don't want Romero to send an army of guards after you, we have to go inside now."

"Okay."

"I'll be with you the whole time." He slid out of the car, buttoned his suit jacket, and then extended his hand for me. "You got this."

I stepped out of the SUV and hooked my arm in his. He had always been my intimating, older cousin. He looked out for me when he could, but his loyalty was with his family. Maybe now that he wasn't who he thought he was, he could be the man he was supposed to be.

Joey's face relaxed when I approached the back door. I was sure my momentary delay caused him plenty of stress. No one wanted to tell my husband they didn't follow his instructions to the letter.

"I'm ready now." I looked at Joey.

Sam and Jag nodded at me as I entered the funeral home. Even from the back room, the place reeked of the aroma of fresh flowers. Most people thought that was a beautiful smell, but I always associated the scent with death. It triggered memories of my parents' funeral. I didn't have a lot of recollection from that day, but the smell of flowers stayed with me.

Rocco approached a man who I assumed was the undertaker. He was a tall, solemn man in a dark suit. He glanced at me and smiled briefly.

"Mrs. Bilotti," he said. "I'm sorry for your loss."

"Thank you," I spoke barely above a whisper. "I don't want to intrude. I just want to say goodbye."

"The visitation is through this hall." He motioned down a long corridor. "There's been a steady stream of people all morning."

Rocco led me down the hall and to the room where Stella rested. There were so many pictures of her through the years.

Her as a child. Several on her wedding day. Lots of photos of her smiling with her children. Vacations, birthdays, anniversaries. My heart hurt as I passed by the memories. She still had so much life to live. Her girls weren't done with school. She wouldn't see them graduate college, get jobs, fall in love, get married, have kids.

"You're trembling," Rocco said.

"I...this is horrible." With each step toward the white, closed casket, my legs became slower. "I can't believe she's in there."

"Breathe." He put his arm around me as we made our way to the casket. "She knows you're here."

"How dare you come here." Stella's husband Mike stood in front of the coffin. "I told your husband I didn't want any of you here."

"I know but I wanted to..."

"I don't care what you want." He pointed at me. "I want my wife back. My children want their mother back. Can you make that happen?"

"No." My face burned as everyone stared at me. "I'm sorry."

I looked at Stella's three girls who were holding one another and crying. I wanted to tell them how much I loved and appreciated their mother, but I didn't want to make things worse.

"Mr. Carone," Rocco said. "I'm very sorry for your loss, but my cousin means no disrespect. Your wife meant a great deal to her, and Stella cared very much for Luciana. Is there any way you could allow her to pay her respects?"

"I'd rather she not." He blocked the path to the casket. "I'd like you both to leave." He looked into my eyes. "If you cared about my wife the way you say you do, you'll leave.

Your presence is nothing but a horrible reminder of what happened to her."

"I understand." My voice shook because his words cut deep. "I'm very sorry for your loss."

I turned, bumping into Rocco as I hurried out of the room, and back down the hallway. Rocco stayed close to my side. I stopped in the corridor and sobbed. I couldn't catch my breath.

"Take a breath," he said.

"I didn't mean to…I just wanted…" I rested my hands on my knees. "I shouldn't have come here."

"I'm sorry that happened." He rubbed my back. "I know he's grieving, but you meant no harm."

"Excuse me, Luciana?" An older man approached us.

"We're leaving," Rocco said. "Just give her a second to catch her breath."

"I'm Stella's father." He extended his hand.

"Oh." I took his hand. "I'm so sorry for your loss."

"Yes." He continued to hold my shaky hand, giving it a gentle squeeze. "She was taken from us way too soon."

I nodded because I didn't know what to say.

"I'm sorry about what happened in there." He motioned toward the room where we had just come from. "My son-in-law is grieving. He's trying to protect his children."

"I should have respected his grief."

"My daughter cared for you, and I know you loved her too." He nodded. "Everyone who knew her did."

"She was very important to me."

"Her death isn't your fault. She knew who Romero was when she accepted the job. He has been generous to our family. He never would have willingly put Stella in a situation like that. I believe that with all of my heart."

"She was bringing me a birthday cake."

"Then she died doing something she wanted to do." He let go of my hand. "Thank you for coming."

"Thank you for finding me." I smiled. "It means a lot."

"I'll reach out to Romero once things settle down and I'll tell him where her plot is so you can visit her whenever you want." He nodded. "She would love the company."

"That would be wonderful." I hugged him. "You raised a strong, amazing woman."

When he let go of me, his eyes were wet, but he smiled through the tears before turning away.

"I'm ready to go now," I said.

"Good." Rocco glanced at his phone. "Someone is waiting for you outside."

"Who?"

"Let's go and see."

I followed Rocco down the hall and to the back room where we entered. When he opened the door, the sunlight poured in, blinding my sight. I reached in my bag and took out my sunglasses as Joey and Sam walked me to the car.

"This way, Lu," Sam said as he led me to the SUV in front of the one we came in.

"Why is Romero's car here?" I asked.

When Joey opened the door, Romero pushed his sunglasses up, revealing his stunning green eyes. "Hello, butterfly."

"What are you doing here?"

"Taking you on an adventure."

CHAPTER 12

Romero

Even with her sunglasses on, I could see she had been crying. I nodded at Rocco. I had already thanked him in a text when I told him I was outside waiting for Lu. Maybe having another brother wasn't such a bad thing.

"Have a safe trip." Rocco headed to his waiting car.

"Thank you for everything," Lu called after him.

"Get in." I scooted over to make room for her. "We have to get to the airport."

"Where are we going?" After she climbed into the SUV, Joey closed the door behind her. "Hi, Salvi."

"Hey, Lu." Salvi waved at her from the driver's seat before pulling onto the street.

"Why are we going to the airport?"

"I have some business to deal with in Italy, so I thought it was a good opportunity for us to get away."

"We're going to Italy?" Her adorable little nose crinkled. "Right now?"

"Right now."

"I don't have anything with me."

"I grabbed some stuff for you, but you can buy whatever you want." I motioned over her black, funeral dress. "I threw some comfortable clothes in your bag for the flight."

"Thank you." Her facial expressions indicated she was still confused. "How did you get us on a flight so fast?"

"Private jet."

"How did you manage that?"

"I know people." I placed her hand in my lap. "Let me worry about all the details. Tell me how it went in there."

She shook her head.

"What happened?" My body tensed when her grief took over her features.

"It was heartbreaking." She squeezed my hand. "You were right. I shouldn't have gone."

"I didn't want to be right." I put my arm around her. "You did what you had to do, and I admire that, but now you have to heal."

"I didn't get to pay my respects." She sighed.

"Why not?"

"They threw me out."

"What?" I clenched my jaw when I thought about the humiliation she must have suffered inside that funeral home. "Who threw you out?"

"Mike."

"That's unacceptable." The thought of anyone hurting her that way blinded me with rage. I realized he was grieving in the worst possible way, but none of this was Luciana's fault. She was hurting too.

"It's okay."

"No, it isn't. You had nothing to do with her death. I understand he's in pain, but to disrespect you that way was not an option."

"I want to forget about it." She rested her head on my

shoulder. "I want to remember Stella the way she was. Vibrant, kind, and caring. These past few days have been a nightmare. I need a break."

"I'm taking you to a quiet, remote villa. We'll be protected there while I figure things out." I kissed the top of her head. "Gio will meet us there in a couple days. He has to take care of things here. You can rest and start to feel better."

"I hope you're right because I'm so tired." She cuddled against me. "I had a dream last night that you ran the club. That was it. That was your job."

"It's a nice dream, baby." I twirled her hair around my finger. "If I could make it come true for you I would."

"Hmm..." She relaxed against me. "Maybe you can. You're a resourceful guy."

My gaze connected with Salvi's in the rearview mirror. He didn't have to say anything, but he was well aware that I would not be a lawful businessman anytime soon. Not if I wanted to keep us all alive.

After a minute or two, her breathing slowed and she seemed calmer. I continued to play with her hair, wondering if she really had a dream or if she wanted me to be legitimate so badly that she thought she dreamt it. Either way, it was never going to happen.

This life was etched in my veins, burned into my soul, and simmered in my blood. There was nothing else for me. This trip would help me reclaim what I had lost. There would be a steep price to pay, but when all was said and done, I would come out on top. No one would ever take a shot at me again.

They wouldn't dare.

After the long flight, and the car ride to the villa, Luciana and I crashed for most of the day. We both needed to catch up on sleep and recharge. After we ate, we went for a walk along the water, taking in the beautiful evening sky.

We decided to stay in tonight, and recoup from the last few days that had turned our lives upside down. A couple weeks in a new setting wouldn't cure all our troubles, but I hoped it would help Luciana heal. She would never forget the drama associated with what had happened to Stella, but with time it would get easier. I wanted to be there for her.

I opened the balcony doors of the master bedroom and gazed out at the ocean. The October air held a refreshing chill. I'd almost forgotten how beautiful the view was from this house. Perhaps I never appreciated it before. I was younger when Gio and I lived here. Luciana wasn't in my life then. She had a way of making me see the beauty in things.

She came out of the bathroom, fresh from the shower. The scent of peppermint swirled between us when she pressed her lips to the top of my shoulder. When she ran her hand across my abs, my erection stirred.

"You have to put the sling back on," she said. "Your shoulder isn't healed."

"I'm tired of the sling." I turned to face her, licking my lips when I took in her damp hair and warm skin. The tan towel clung to her body, but it wasn't going to stay there for long. "I'll put it back on after."

"After what?" She traced her finger along the tattoos on my chest.

"After we take this off." I tugged on her towel, letting it fall to the floor. "That's better."

"But now I'm naked and you're not." She trailed her fingers down my stomach. "That doesn't seem fair."

"How about I decide what's fair?" I kissed the side of her

jaw, working my way down her throat, and to her breasts. "I like being in charge."

"Really?" She giggled, and that was probably the first time she smiled in days. "I haven't noticed."

"Turn around." I moved her to face the balcony "You should enjoy the view."

"Won't someone see us?"

"No." I kissed the back of her neck, breathing in her peppermint shampoo as I roamed my hands up her sides and to her breasts. "We're too high up on the cliff, but I wouldn't care who sees me fucking you."

"Oh…" she moaned when I swiveled my hips into her back side.

I inched us forward until we were outside, overlooking the ocean. The sound of the water crashed in the distance, and the air was filled with a crisp autumn aroma.

I cupped her breasts, pinching her nipples between my fingers, tugging on them. The cool breeze from the open patio doors swept along my heated flesh. I lowered one hand between her legs, pushing my fingers inside her, and spreading her arousal along her folds.

She gripped the black iron railing that surrounded the balcony as I fingered her. Her walls clenched around me, alerting me to her impending climax. She arched her hips and rocked into my hand. I kissed the side of her neck, licking a path to her ear.

"Fuck my fingers, my dirty girl." I swirled my tongue inside her ear, gently blowing inside it. "When you're done, I'm going to suck your cum from them."

"You're filthy."

"You like it."

"Yes." She panted, leaning forward. "Romero…"

She unraveled under my touch, clutching the railing as

her legs quivered and she tightened around my fingers. I withdrew my hand from between her legs, dragging it along her ass and up her spine.

Still leaning against the railing, she glanced over her shoulder and locked her gaze with mine when I brought my fingers to my lips and tasted her juices. If I wasn't so hard for her, I'd drop to my knees and feast on her, but my cock had other ideas.

I lowered my sweatpants over my waist, freeing my erection. She ran her tongue along her lips when she turned to face me, taking my length in her palm and stroking it. I took her face between my hands and pushed my tongue into her mouth. As our teeth collided in a frenzied attempt for control, she pumped me in her delicate hand.

She breathlessly broke the kiss, staring at me with wild eyes. In that moment, I saw a flicker of hope in them. When she released me from her hold, I turned her to face the ocean again. I flexed my waist forward, pushing my cock between the soft skin of her legs, rubbing myself against her as I bit the top of her shoulder.

She pushed back, moving with me, coating my shaft with the dampness of her pussy. I guided her to lean against the balcony, and arched her hips as I took my length in my hand and ran the tip along her entrance, savoring the warmth.

She braced herself against the railing, holding tight as I plunged inside her. As much as I stretched her, she was still tight around me. Her hot, wet core welcomed me, allowing me to move slow and deep. With a shove forward, my balls slapped against her ass. My lust for her grew stronger with each pass of her swollen folds.

As the waves broke to the surf in the distance, we created our own nature. Just she and I, needing one another, pleasing each other until all our pain and grief faded to the background. She hadn't been this relaxed in days. She needed this; she needed me.

With my one hand on her hip, I placed my other on top of one of hers, interlacing our fingers. The light of the moon illuminated over us, bouncing off the ocean below. I slowed my tempo because I didn't want this to end.

"I love you so much," I whispered into her ear. "I'll make things better, I promise."

"I love you." She tightened her grip on my hand. "I trust you."

"Lu..." I moaned as I rocked my pelvis and emptied inside her.

"Oh!" She cried out when I glided my hand up her stomach and to her throat, gently holding it as I brought her to release a second time tonight.

She slouched against the railing, trying to catch her breath. I covered her with my body, embracing her. I ignored the pain in my shoulder because this encounter far out-weighted any discomfort I experienced. Being close to her was the only support I needed.

"I think I'm going to like it here," she said. "The view is spectacular."

"I thought you might like it."

"Can we go down there and have a picnic?"

"Now?"

"No." When she laughed, I smiled. "Tomorrow."

"Whatever you want." I kissed her neck. "I'll give you anything you want."

That wasn't completely true, because the most important thing she wanted, I couldn't give her. A life free of violence and death. A world where she could go outside by herself, drive to a store alone, go out and get a cup of coffee.

None of those things other people took for granted were in Luciana's future. Not as long as she stayed with me.

"Hey." She looked over her shoulder. "Where did you go?"

"Huh?"

"You're a million miles away."

"I'm right here." I trailed my hand down her back. "Let's go inside."

As I guided her back into the bedroom, I picked her towel up from the floor and wrapped her in it. When she looked up at me with her beautiful, innocent eyes, I promised myself I wouldn't have any more dark thoughts tonight.

I came here to fix what was wrong back in New York. If I had to sell my soul to do that, I would do whatever it took to keep my wife safe and by my side.

Could I do both?

CHAPTER 13

Luciana

Romero and I finished dinner on the covered patio. The stone pillars accentuated the marble floors that flowed throughout the large area. It was located off the kitchen, giving the staff easy access to and from the patio. When dinner was over, they cleared the table, and left us for the evening.

We cuddled on a chaise lounge in front of a built-in fireplace that helped to warm the chilly October evening. I rested under his good arm as I laid my head on his chest. I almost felt like myself again.

"This house is fantastic." I looked up at the painted ceilings. "How were you able to rent it on such short notice?"

"I didn't rent it." He twirled my hair around his fingers. "I own it."

"This is your place?"

"It's *our* place, and Gio's." He continued to play with my hair. "We lived here after our father died. It was originally his house. We haven't been back in two years, but we let friends and associates use it from time to time."

"Why don't you come here more often?"

"You mean, why have I never taken you here?" He laughed. "That's a good question."

"It's just so beautiful. I would think you'd want to visit more often."

There was much I still didn't know about my husband. Some things I didn't want to know, but there were other details I craved to learn.

"I didn't mean to stay away for so long, but when Gio and I came to New York we were busy making a name for ourselves. There wasn't time to come back here. Then, you and I got together, and I was busy fighting with your family."

"We should have fled to Italy."

"Well, now that I know you like it here, I'll take you back often."

"It's not any different here than it is at home, is it?" We came here because he needed help with the problems at home. "With your business."

"This is where I got my start," he said. "There's a strong organized crime presence. I have more allies here than I do in the states at the moment. Some would say these men are more brutal than what I deal with at home."

"Would you say that?"

"I learned plenty from them."

"I don't understand how you do this every day, especially after what happened to Stella." I didn't think I would ever be able to go back to our house. "Doesn't it bother you?"

"Does what happened to Stella bother me? How could you ask me that? You know it does." The tone in his voice changed, and now I'd put him in a defensive mood. "She was my friend for a long time. I asked her to come into my home and work for me. If I had believed for a second that someone would murder her in cold-blood, do you think I would have put her in that situation?"

"I don't believe you would have put her in danger, but she was in danger."

"In all of the years you spent with your uncle, did you ever feel threatened by outside forces?"

"No, but we had guards and no one could get near the house if they weren't supposed to be there." I thought for a moment. "But, we have that too. How did Stella become a target?"

"She was in the wrong place at the wrong time." He tightened his hold on me. "The point is, there is supposed to be a code. We don't go after innocent people. At least, we never did before. We have guards for protection, but honorable men don't go after innocent women. That's why I'm here. I need to find out what's going on and I need the people who run this territory to help me."

"But at what cost to you?"

"You let me worry about my business." He kissed the top of my head. "You have enough on your plate with school and dealing with your grief."

"I worry about you." I sat up and faced him. "I worry something will happen to you."

"Baby, I've been taking care of myself for a long time. I'm reckless and impulsive, but I'm smart." He cupped the side of my face. "Now that you're my wife, I have more reason to be careful. I'm not leaving you, and I promise, whoever tried to kill me is going to pay in ways they never imagined."

That's what worries me.

"Hey, you're too beautiful for this conversation. You don't need to know the details of my business." He guided me onto his lap and positioned my legs on either side of his hips. "I can think of other ways to spend our time." He slipped his hands up my thighs and under my dress, grasping my waist and moving me up and down over his erection.

"Mmm..." I lowered my lips to his as I trailed my hands down his chest.

The more he moved me against him, the wetter I became. There was never a time when I didn't want my husband, and tonight was no exception, but I had to be responsible. I slipped my hands down his stomach and to his belt buckle. He tugged on my panties, indicating he wanted them off, but I ignored his silent request, and continued my mission. I shimmied down his body, and unbuttoned his pants, looking up at him through the hair that had fallen in my face as I drew down his zipper.

"You're so fucking sexy." He glided his fingers through my hair as I took his length in my hand.

"Lu..." he moaned when I swirled my tongue around his tip, tasting the salty liquid that had beaded there.

He tugged on my hair as he rested his head on the back of the chair, shifting his hips forward, allowing me to take more of him. I fit as much as I could into my mouth, relaxing my throat when he pushed forward. I gripped the base, squeezing and pumping him in my palm.

His leg muscles tensed beneath me and the veins in his neck and chest stretched under his skin. When I cradled his balls in my other hand and continued to suck him off, he let go of my hair and tugged on my upper arm.

"What?" I licked my lips. "I'm not done."

"No." He pulled me up the length of his body. "We aren't done." As he kissed me, he reached under my dress and tugged on my panties. "Take them off."

"I want to but..." I kissed his mouth, rubbing my hand over his shaft. "Let me do this for you."

"We can do it to one another." He shoved his tongue inside my mouth, kissing me so hard the stubble on his jaw scraped against my chin. "I want to get inside you." He gripped the side of my panties and yanked at them, ripping them from me. "Right now."

"No." I pushed against his chest, but he continued to kiss me.

"You know I don't care if you have your period." He ran his hand along my backside. "Do you need a minute to use the bathroom?"

"No, that's the thing." I kissed him back because I didn't want to resist him, but I had to tell him. "I've been lax with my pill with all that's going on, and I need to get that sorted out before we...well...you know."

When we had sex two nights ago, I wasn't ovulating, but now it was getting too close to that time, and I shouldn't be so careless. After Stella died, there were days when I had skipped doses. I tried to remember, but my head wasn't in the right place.

"What if we don't get it sorted out?" He caressed my face. "Would that be such a bad thing?"

"What do you mean?"

"What do you think I mean?"

"Umm...we're not ready for that." Did he seriously want to have this conversation now? "We can't have a baby."

"I'm pretty sure we can, but why not?" He sat up and somehow managed to tuck himself back into his pants and zipper them with one hand.

"This isn't the right time." I lived in constant fear now that Stella had been murdered in our home. Did he really believe bringing a baby into our lives was a good idea? "I just started school, and you're running the club and, well, your other business. We can't have a baby."

"We can't or you don't want to?" He stood and walked to the bar cart in the corner of the patio, and then poured himself a drink. "Tell me, Luciana, do you want to have a child with me?"

"Yes, eventually." I joined him by the bar cart. "When the time is right."

"When do you think that will be?" He sipped his drink, never taking his eyes away from me. How did those beautiful green eyes filled with such desire for me a few minutes ago turn dark and frightening?

"I don't know."

"You better come up with some kind of explanation."

"We never discussed this before." I waved my hand in the air. "And with everything going on, now isn't really the time to have this conversation."

"You're my wife. I just assumed you wanted to have a family with me."

"I do, but not now." I didn't understand where he was coming from. "It's no secret that I've been on birth control all this time. We had sex the other night because I needed you, but I shouldn't have been careless. I stopped us tonight because you needed to know I missed a few doses."

"That fact that you skipped some pills changes nothing for me. If you getting pregnant is meant to be then I don't see what the problem is."

"We have a lot of problems." I had been trying to hold my shit together for days but I could only take so much. "You were shot, Stella was killed in our home, I wasn't welcomed at her funeral because I'm your wife. My cousin drugged and kidnapped me. Am I missing anything?"

My body shook with frustration and anxiety. How much more could I endure before I snapped?

"You left out the part that you are fucking married to an

arms dealer who kills people for a living and that's never going to change." He finished his drink and slammed the glass down on the cart. "That's what this is really about."

"I don't want to fight with you."

"Then maybe you shouldn't have killed the mood between us."

"That's what you're concerned with?" I shouted because now my emotions were all over the place. "I didn't say I didn't want to be with you. I just didn't want to have sex. We can be intimate in other ways and still be close to one another. I only wanted to situate my cycle and get back on track."

"Because you don't want to have a baby with me."

"That isn't what I said."

"It's what you meant."

When he took a step toward me, I moved away from him.

"That's fucking great, Lu. You're back to retreating. When am I ever going to be good enough for you?"

"You're overreacting." My tears betrayed me as they streamed down my cheeks. "We've both been through so much trauma this last week. We need to heal and come to terms with the violence that surrounds us. I want to do that as a couple. We need to be together."

"We can't do that unless you start accepting and understanding who I am. Who you married. Until you do that, we're further apart than I ever imagined."

"You're reading too much into this."

"Am I?" He took the bottle of vodka from the cart. "Did I read too much into your dream the other night? The one where I'm the legitimate businessman that you so desperately need me to be. The husband you could have chosen if you could have picked for yourself?"

"Romero."

"Would you be ready to have a baby with him?"

Before I could answer, he went inside with the vodka. It was probably best if I didn't try and finish this conversation tonight. I had no idea that suggesting we hold off on having a baby would cause so much hurt and anger. We had never discussed children before. We weren't even married that long.

I plopped down on the chaise lounge, wondering how this night had gone so wrong. I rested my head on the cushions and closed my eyes. I would give him some time to cool down. We could discuss this more rationally when we both weren't so emotionally charged.

CHAPTER 14

Romero

"Fuck!" I fought through the pain in my shoulder to get my suit jacket on. It was difficult to maneuver my arm in that position, but I needed to get dressed.

"Let me help you." Luciana came up from behind me and pulled the jacket up over my shoulder while I slipped my arm through the sleeve. "We probably should have put the sling on first."

"I'm not wearing the sling." I turned around to find her still wearing the dress she had on when I left her on the patio last night. "It's a sign of weakness, and I have an important meeting."

"Today?"

"That's why I'm here." I took my gun out of the top dresser drawer and secured it behind my waistband in my pants. "Where did you sleep last night?"

My head pounded from the vodka. I had passed out on the bed and slept straight through until morning. I didn't realize she wasn't in bed until I reached for her and she wasn't there. Her absence did nothing good for my foul mood.

"Were you afraid I would impregnate you if you slept in the same bed as me?"

"I wanted to give you time to cool down, but I fell asleep on the patio. I guess I was exhausted." She sat on the edge of the bed. "I can see you're still upset with me."

I didn't respond. Her observation didn't need one.

"This meeting," she said. "Is it dangerous?"

"No more dangerous than every other day."

"That doesn't put my mind at ease."

"I don't know what you want me to say. Would you rather me lie?"

I didn't know why the conversation last night had left me so miserable. It wasn't as if we had talked about having kids anytime soon. Luciana was barely into her twenties. I wanted her to finish school. We needed time to become a couple. To have our own experiences before we brought a baby into our lives.

Where was all that rational thinking last night?

"Romero." Gio called from down the stairs. "We're going to be late."

"Gio is here?" Lu asked.

"He arrived a few hours ago." I nodded toward the bedroom door. "We'll talk later."

She followed me into the hallway and down the open staircase to the foyer where Gio waited for me.

"Hi, Lu," my brother said. "Are you enjoying Italy?"

"I haven't seen much, but this house is spectacular." When she came to stand next to me, our arms touched one another's, but I had to resist touching her. "We had a picnic on the beach."

"How romantic." Gio smirked at me. "Maybe we can do a

little sight-seeing now that I'm here. You know, give you a break from the bedroom." He winked at me. "We have to go."

Ass.

"When will you be back?" Lu asked.

"I don't know." I moved toward the door when Gio opened it.

"Joey and Salvi are coming with us," Gio said. "Sam and Jag will stay with Lu."

"Don't leave the property," I said to Luciana. "If you want to walk on the beach take Sam with you."

"I have school work to do," she said. "I'll probably just hang out on the patio."

"Your new favorite place." I stepped outside, but she didn't follow. "We'll be home later."

When I turned to shut the door, the look in her eyes was enough to make me fall to my knees. The hurt etched in her expression would haunt me for the rest of the day, but I wasn't ready to forget about our previous conversation.

"I see you and Lu are getting along." Gio opened the car door and climbed into the backseat. "What did you do to her?"

"Fuck off." I got in and slammed the door. "Why is it that I had to have done something?"

"Because you have a temper." He shrugged. "Usually you're all over her, but you didn't even kiss her goodbye. You probably hurt her feelings."

"We had a stupid argument and it escalated. She never came to bed last night."

"So, then the argument was your fault."

"I don't think it was." I rested my head against the seat. "Maybe it was."

"What happened?"

"The topic of having kids came up."

"Lu wants to have a baby?"

"Not exactly." I glanced at my phone, hoping she would give in and text me. "She doesn't think now is the right time."

"And you disagree?"

"No."

"Why are you mad?"

"She's right, the timing for us to have a baby is off, but she doesn't think I can keep her safe, and that pisses me off. If I can't keep her safe, how can I keep a kid safe?"

"She's upset about Stella," Gio said. "You have to give her time to mourn."

"I know, but she's not wrong. It's just that when she said it out loud, it bothered me. I said some things that I shouldn't have."

"I'm shocked." He rolled his eyes.

"Shut up."

"When you and Lu are ready to start a family, you'll do everything in your power to protect her and your children. What happened with Stella was awful, but that's not how our business works. Whoever is responsible for doing such a horrible thing, well, it feels really personal to me."

"You don't think it has to do with our line of work?"

"I'm sure it does, but I've been thinking about it and checking some things out. The cartel has stopped all of us from moving products in and out of the city. We're all at a stand-still because we know if we cross them, they hit back harder."

"There would have been no reason to come at us, unless they were being proactive. Maybe Stella's death was a warning."

"Perhaps, but why go after her? Why take a shot at us and miss? It seems a little sloppy."

"I wondered how we escaped the bullets that day too. They had a clear shot at me but hit me in the shoulder." If whoever targeted me wanted me dead, I would be dead. "How are things at home?"

"Everyone is still laying low." Gio took out a pack of gum and offered me a stick.

I shook my head.

"The ports are quiet. Business is suffering."

"We have to put a stop to that," I said. "I'm hoping this meeting with Malatesta helps."

"I'm sure he can help." Gio glanced out the window. "But what is it going to cost us?"

"At this point, I'm willing to pay any price."

⁓

THIRTY MINUTES LATER, we were at a sprawling, secluded estate owned by Italy's most influential mafia boss. Janero Malatesta was as old-school as they came. He was brutal, relentless, and always got what he wanted. He was a formidable enemy, but an ally anyone in my position would be lucky to have. I hoped I could still consider him that.

He had been close to our father, and after his death he took me and Gio under his wing. He protected us while we learned the business. He respected our decision not to take over the New York territory our father had left vacant when he was murdered. Instead, he let me find my way. He guided me when I needed his expertise, but I didn't want any special favors from him. Ten years ago, I had a lot to prove, and if I wanted to make a name for myself, I had to get there on my own.

When we arrived, we handed over our guns as a show of good faith and let the guards frisk us. We had nothing to hide. We weren't here to come after Janero, and they knew it, but they had a job to do. If I wanted Janero's help, I had to play by his rules.

When we entered the grand foyer covered in marble from floor to ceiling, we were greeted by a beautiful young woman. I stared at her for a moment, taking in her wide brown eyes, and delicate frame. Her olive skin glowed in the sunlight streaming from the stain-glass windows.

"Is that Janero's daughter?" I asked.

Gio seemed to be too mesmerized to respond.

"Ciao." She approached us.

"Cinzia?" Gio asked.

"Si, Gio, Si." She took his hands in hers, gracing him with an innocent smile. "It's been a long two years."

"I...wow!" Gio kissed her cheeks. "How old are you now?"

"Venti." She laughed. "I just turned twenty."

At least she's legal.

"Your English has improved." Gio let go of her hands. "Impressive."

"I studied what you taught me." She looked at me. "Hello, Romero."

"Cinzia." I nodded. "E'bello vederti."

"It's good to see you too." She pointed down the hallway to her father's study. "Papa is expecting you."

As we followed her down the long hallway, Gio couldn't take his eyes off her.

"Did you teach her anything besides English?" I whispered.

"She was a kid when we left."

"She's definitely not a kid now."

Cinzia glanced over her shoulder and smiled at my brother with her full pink lips. She seemed to be just as taken with Gio as he was with her.

I needed to get this meeting with her father over with before Gio screwed things up by screwing the Don's daughter.

When we approached the study door, Janero was already waiting for us. He was a tall man with an imposing figure. He had aged well. Even with a head full of silver hair, he appeared youthful, but his eyes were old. Maybe not with wrinkles, but he had seen plenty in his fifty-five years.

"The Bilotti brothers are here," she said. "Do you need me to get you anything?"

"We're fine." He kissed her cheek. "Leave us now."

She glanced at Gio before hurrying down the hall. I moved into Gio's line of sight, blocking his view of Cinzia when I noticed he lingered on her a little too long. Lusting after her in front of her father wasn't the smartest thing he could do.

He would have no qualms over shooting Gio in the head for being inappropriate where his daughter was concerned. That was a war I didn't need.

"Don Malatesta." I cleared my throat, trying to get Gio back on track. "Thank you for seeing us today."

"Romero, how is your recovery going?" Janero shook my hand. "Such an unfortunate mishap."

"I'm doing well. It's just a small injury," I assured him. "It's not a problem."

"It sounds like you have several problems. You should have requested a meeting with me months ago."

"I didn't want to disturb you, but now I could use your help." I hated to admit that, but I didn't have a choice.

"You could have used my help before Giancarlo talked

you into an alliance with the man who murdered your father." Janero's jaw tightened. "I know that's never been proven, but whether Antonio pulled the trigger himself, or he had someone do it, he stepped into your father's place. Your rightful place."

"I didn't come here to discuss history." I never wanted to avenge my father's death, but Antonio wouldn't be on top forever.

"If it isn't the man who taught my daughter English. Now she insists I don't speak to her in Italian." Janero patted Gio's back. "I guess I have you to thank for her begging me to visit America."

"Cinzia wants to come to America?" Gio asked. "I would love for her to visit."

I'm sure you would.

"Let's see how this meeting goes." He motioned for us to enter his study, and then he shut the door. "Maybe I'll allow her to visit you. She was very excited that you were coming today."

"She's stunning," Gio said. "You must be very protective of her."

"You have no idea." He rolled his eyes. "I'm constantly approached by other families looking to make an alliance and marry into this family." Janero looked at me. "You know all about that, don't you?"

"I do."

"How is your wife?" He motioned for me to have a seat in front of his desk.

"She's well." I took a seat on the sofa. "She's enjoying your country."

"She's grieving," he said. "Gio told me she was close to your friend."

"Stella's death has been tough on all of us, but it has hit

Luciana the hardest," I said. "It was senseless and put us in a vulnerable position."

"Yes, I agree." He sat at his desk. "Having your home attacked makes you vulnerable."

"That's why we're here." I glanced at Gio who chose to stand behind the sofa. "My business has been paralyzed. The cartel doesn't trust me because of the agreement I entered into with the Torrios."

"They don't trust you because Antonio got the better of you, but when you blew up his warehouse, you put yourself back in a position of strength."

"I've made some mistakes," I admitted.

"New York is a mess," he said. "But the cartel is not the problem."

"They aren't?" Gio questioned. "What do you think the problem is?"

"Weak leadership." He nodded. "I believe the cartel was responsible for the botched attempt on you and Romero. They were also responsible for the hit on LaVanza's son."

"You're sure?" I asked.

"I have it on good authority, but the cartel can't be blamed. They have to do what they have to do to protect their assets."

"I was protecting their assets," I said. "Until Antonio fucked me over."

"I don't see anyone in power strong enough to lead right now." Janero shook his head. "The Torrios house is not in order. Antonio's three sons are no longer working as a united front. They are distracted."

"You're right." Gio nodded at me. "They are divided."

"I don't care what their issues are," he said. "I only want to use them as an advantage. The Marchelli family is strong, but Dante doesn't seem interested in this life any more. Two

His Broken Queen

of his sons are legitimate. The other three have potential, but they don't seem to want total control of the city. They have other sources of income." He leaned back in his chair. "The LaVanza family has been dealt three tragic blows in the last few months. They are not capable of running things."

"From where you're sitting," I said. "It does seem pretty bleak, but I think we can get things back on track."

"I do too." He stared at me. "There's an emerging family I'm quite interested in. I have been from the time they realized who they wanted to become."

"You want a new family to take over?" Gio asked.

"They're not exactly new." Janero pointed at me. "It's time for you to step up and take your rightful place in this organization."

"You know I don't want that," I said. "I never wanted to be in charge of all of it. I only wanted to expand my business and move my product."

"How is that working out for you?" Janero slammed his fist on his desk. "I let you find your way when you wanted to go to the states. I didn't interfere when you started working with the cartel. It was lucrative and a smart deal until it wasn't. I stood by and watched you get into bed with the Torrios because I respected your choice to become your own man, but now you're here for my help, and I'll give it to you, but it has to come at a cost."

"I'm not here for charity."

"The city is ripe for a takeover. I can help you, but I'll expect your total allegiance."

"I wouldn't ask you for your help if I wasn't willing to repay you."

"You know my price will be steep."

"I do, but I'm sure it will be worth it." I had to find a way to keep my business going while I protected Luciana and Gio.

"Are you saying you want Romero to take over in exchange for your help?" Gio joined me on the sofa.

"That's just the beginning, Gio, but don't worry, I have plans for you too." He smirked. "In order for Romero to take charge of the New York territory, you have to get back in business."

"That's why I'm here," I said. "I need you to help me figure out how to let the cartel allow me to move my product."

"Fuck the cartel," Janero scoffed. "They answer to me."

"When did that happen?"

"When I took down a major player in their organization. The new regime needed my help and in exchange, I call the shots."

"What do I have to do?" There was no turning back now.

"There's going to be a change with the Feds in the city, so now is the time to strike. No one will be looking. I haven't infiltrated New York because I didn't want to upset the balance there, but now that things aren't moving at all, I need to step in and take charge. When one of us loses money, we all lose money." He stood and came around his desk. "If you help me, I'll see to it that you start moving your product as soon as you return home. You'll be in charge of the ports. I'll make sure of that."

"And the cartel?" I asked.

"They won't be a problem for you any longer. I'll make sure they are handled and well-compensated. You will have control. You'll decide who you allow to move merchandise in and out of the city. You and Gio will run the day-to-day operations there." He leaned against his desk. "You'll have my total protection and full support. I don't have a long-term interest in the city. It will eventually be yours."

"What's in it for you?" I placed my hands on my thighs. "Not that I don't appreciate all of this, especially since I've managed to screw things up so quickly."

"You trusted your father's second." He shrugged. "I have a feeling Giancarlo is no longer a problem."

"You could say that."

"That's because you are smart and you know what has to be done. Making a deal with the Torrios was a solid plan, but they double-crossed you. Now you'll have the leverage to stop them in their tracks."

Gio shifted in his seat, and I wouldn't be surprised if he was worried that Rocco would get caught in the middle of this. He definitely could, but that wasn't my concern right now. I had an empire to fix.

"I need a fresh place to launder some cash," Janero said. "I need someone who I trust completely. Someone I know would never betray me."

"Gio and I owe you our lives," I said. "We will do what you need."

"Even if it means your totally legitimate club is the perfect place for you to launder my money?" Janero studied my expression. "Because that's my price."

CHAPTER 15

*L*uciana

"I win!" I raised my arms in triumph. "That's three games in a row."

"You always were the Rummy queen." Sam gathered up the cards. "You still got it."

"I missed this." I smiled because for a couple hours Sam had managed to get my mind off that stupid disagreement I had with Romero. "I'm so glad you're here."

"I am too, Lu." He pushed the stack of cards back into the box. "After that night Romero had to come and get you, I realized I didn't belong with the Torrios. My place was with you."

"What you did to protect me that night was difficult, but if you would have alerted Vincent or the other guards things could have been really different."

"Romero would have killed me before he let anything happen to you. Besides, it's always been my job to protect you, no matter who I work for." He set the cards down on the patio table. "When Romero asked me to come and work for him, I could see how much you meant to him."

I nodded before taking a sip of my iced tea, trying not to remember how hurt he was last night. When he left today, he didn't kiss me goodbye. That gutted me.

"Is everything okay?" Sam asked.

"Yeah, it's been a crazy few days. I'm drained and emotional, and I think it's taking a toll on Romero."

"Romero can handle your emotions," Sam said. "You suffered a traumatic loss. You are entitled to feel how you feel. I've been with you a long time. Things haven't always been easy for you, but you're a fighter."

"I'm tired."

"You're going to get through this." He reached across the table and placed his hand on mine. "You're finally where you belong."

"I'm going to have to agree with you, Sam." Romero leaned against the arch that joined the patio to the hall. He looked as impeccable as he had when he left hours earlier, but there was something off in his gaze. "Playing cards?"

"Your wife is a real shark." Sam stood. "She never lets me win."

"I didn't know you could play cards." Romero joined us on the patio. "I learn something new about you every day."

Did he mean that as a compliment?

"I'll leave you two alone," Sam said.

"Thanks for keeping me company." I waved as he left through the kitchen.

Romero headed to the bar cart and fixed himself a drink. The staff must have replaced the bottle he took with him to bed last night. He rattled the ice around in his glass before taking a long, slow sip.

"Did Sam teach you how to play cards?" He staggered toward me with the glass and the bottle. He didn't appear to need any more alcohol this afternoon.

"Vincent, Rocco, and Sandro would never let me play. Sam felt bad for me, so on Friday nights we would have a tournament."

"I'm glad he's back with you."

"Me too." I ran my finger around the rim of my glass. "I appreciate you doing that for me."

"I would do anything for you." He took another drink before pouring more vodka into his glass. "Don't you know that?"

"I do."

"Good."

"Where's Gio?"

"He stayed behind. Something caught his eye at our meeting."

"He met a woman?"

"We already knew her. She's the daughter of Janero Malatesta, an extremely powerful and influential person in my line of work. He was good to me when I was a kid. Now he's going to be even better to me as an adult. Because of him, we can go back to the states in a few days, and I can resume my business."

"Just like that?"

"What are you asking me?"

"It seems like you would have to sell your soul to a man like that." What did he promise in exchange for such a huge favor?

"It wasn't cheap." He took another long sip, closing his eyes and letting the alcohol do its job. "But whose soul is?"

"I hope it was worth it," I mumbled. I wouldn't bother asking him the details, because he wouldn't tell me, and I probably didn't want to know.

"I don't do anything if it isn't worth it." He smirked.

His Broken Queen

"Look what that alliance with your uncle cost me, but I would still say it was worth it."

"Would you?"

"Why would you say that?" When he slammed the glass down on the table, some of the vodka spilled out. "I have never regretted marrying you, not even when..." He shook his head. "Never mind."

"Not even when I betrayed you?" Would he ever truly forgive me for that? Maybe I didn't deserve forgiveness.

"I wasn't going to say that."

"Then what were you going to say?"

"Not even when you said you didn't want to have my child." He finished his drink. "That hurt me more than your betrayal ever could."

"I didn't mean to hurt you." How could I explain this to him without making this whole misunderstanding worse? "I didn't say I never wanted to have a baby with you."

"I get it, Lu." He gripped the neck of the bottle. "You're right, this isn't the time to have a baby, but hearing you say it somehow made me feel like I'm a failure. Less of a man because you don't think I can protect our family."

"I don't think that. This has nothing to do with protecting me."

"Tell me what you do think." He poured another glass of vodka. "I need to know."

"Maybe you should slow down." I pointed to his glass. "You look like you've had enough today." I had never seen him this drunk before. He didn't relinquish control that easily.

"It's been a long day and my shoulder hurts." He pressed the glass to his lips and drank half of what he had poured into it. "Don't avoid this conversation."

"The honest truth is, I'm not ready to have a baby. I want

us first. If that sounds selfish, I'm sorry, but it's how I feel. I didn't mean to hurt you. You're everything to me."

"I want to have children with you." He twisted his wedding band around his finger. "I know this isn't the time. I'm sorry I acted the way I did. I have so much on my mind. It's no excuse, but I blew what you said out of proportion and only heard what I thought you were saying. I should have stayed and listened."

"Our relationship is still new, and I love us." I reached across the table and took his hand. "You're already an amazing husband. I can only imagine the fantastic father you'll be when the time comes."

"Come here." He tugged on my arm until I got up and came to him. He guided me into his lap. "I'm a jerk."

"Sometimes." I buried my head in the crook of his neck. "But you're my jerk."

"I'll help you get your prescription situated tomorrow." He rubbed my back. "I speak the language here, so I'll sort it out for you. We can get the doctor to transfer it here."

"Thank you." I kissed his jaw. "You said we could go home. How soon?"

"Are you ready to leave?"

"No." I cuddled into his chest. "We just got here."

"We can stay longer." He wrapped his arms around me. "I have some business to deal with. It's probably better if we lay low for a bit anyway. Just until I have a plan in place." He tilted my chin and stared into my eyes. "I don't want you to worry though, you're not in danger." He gently kissed me. "I'll take you shopping tomorrow."

"I don't need anything."

"That's not true." He kissed me again, this time he lingered at my lips a little longer, making me warm and fuzzy. "Italian designers are the best. You need a new bag and shoes, I'm sure of it. I want a new suit."

"You have a hundred suits."

"So, now I'll have a hundred and one." He laughed, causing the tension in his face to disappear. "I may not have given you the wedding you wanted, but I can give you a honeymoon." He closed his eyes. "Right now, I need to go to bed. I drank too much today."

"Did you eat anything?" I scooted off his lap. "I can make you something."

"Maybe later." He took my hand and let me help him up. "Will you lay down with me?"

"Yes." I put his arm around me for support and walked him into the house. "Can you make it upstairs?"

"I'm not that drunk." He knocked into me. "Sorry."

"You were saying?" I laughed. "One step at a time."

"Okay." He climbed the stairs, stopping about every two to check his balance.

"I got you."

"I'm supposed to have you." He held onto me. "And let's face it, if I fall, I'm probably going to take you with me."

"Then don't fall."

We continued up the stairs and to the bedroom. Once inside, he leaned against the wall as I shut the door. I'd never seen him lose his composure after drinking. He could hold his alcohol, so whatever he gave up today in exchange for Malatesta's help must have been a big deal.

"Are you okay?" I helped him out of his jacket.

He closed his eyes and fought through the pain when I shimmied it over his injured shoulder.

"Sorry." I kissed him.

"It's all right." He stepped out of his shoes, and took off his socks.

As I unbuttoned his shirt, he ran his fingers through my hair, twisting it around his hand, and bringing my lips to his. Our mouths barely touched, but his warm breath made me tingle with excitement. Staring into his gorgeous eyes, I spread his shirt open.

"Are you ready?" I inched the shirt down his shoulders, taking his good arm out of the first sleeve. He pushed away from the wall, and wiggled out of the other sleeve.

"I need more vodka." He breathed out. "It fucking hurts."

"You need a nap."

"I need you." He tugged me against his bare chest, and claimed my mouth, kissing me with so much force, I had to hold on to him.

"Let's get you into bed."

"You're not finished undressing me." His smug half-smile made him irresistible. "I can't go to bed with my pants on."

"Of course not." I smoothed my hands down his chest and over his rock-hard abs. When I got to his belt buckle, I noticed his abs weren't the only thing that were rock hard.

"I like when you undress me." He tucked my hair behind my ear. "We're going to have to work that into our rotation."

"You're always so eager to get my clothes off." Most of the time we had sex with his pants down around his hips because he couldn't wait. "Undressing you is kind of nice."

I unbuttoned his pants, but when I went to unzip them, he stopped me. I looked up at him with a questioning gaze.

"My gun." He turned around so I could see the shiny metal sticking out from the back of his pants.

I hesitated because I wasn't comfortable handling a weapon.

He glanced over his shoulder, his intoxicated eyes getting sleepy. "What's wrong?"

"I don't ..."

"Oh, right." He removed his gun, and turned back around. "When we get back home, I'm going to teach you to shoot. It's not a bad skill to have. I'll make sure you learn the proper way."

He moved toward the dresser, and set the gun on top. When he took off his pants, he fell into the wall.

"Romero." I stood next to him.

"I love you." He pressed his palm against my cheek. "Everything is going to be okay."

"I trust you." I leaned into his touch. "I always will."

"I hope you mean that." He kissed my forehead. "Everything I did today was for you. For us."

"What did you do?"

"Secured our future." He took my hand and led me to the bed. "You don't have to worry about it."

He dropped onto the pillows, pulling me down next to him. When he cradled me in his good arm, I rested my head on his chest. I craved being close to him.

"Stay with me." He held me tight. "Promise you'll never leave me."

"I promise," I whispered.

"I'm not a bad person, Lu," he mumbled. "Sometimes, I have to do bad things."

As his breathing slowed and he let sleep take over, I didn't move from his hold. He would probably never tell me what he had to do to get the help of the man he went to see. It was better that I didn't know because if I knew there was a pretty chance my deepest dream would never come true. The one where we lived in peace with our beautiful children. I would never have to fear for our lives.

For better or worse, I loved him.

CHAPTER 16

Romero

"I can't believe you let me talk you into it." I trailed my fingers along her arm. "It's very sexy."

"It didn't hurt as much as I thought."

"Baby, I thought you were going to pass out."

"I wasn't that bad."

"When you weren't screaming."

"It was a sensitive spot." She flipped her wrist over and admired her new butterfly tattoo that said *his* underneath it. "Let me see yours."

I rested my forearm next to her arm and put our matching tattoos next to one another. Mine was bigger and said *hers* under it. She took a picture of them and smiled.

"I love them."

"Me too." I clasped her hand in mine as we cuddled on the bed after an afternoon of making love.

The rain pelted against the windows on this damp, dreary day. After we got our tattoos, we decided to come home and retreat to the bedroom. Tonight was our last night in Italy.

His Broken Queen

"I can't believe we're leaving tomorrow," she said. "These last two weeks have been wonderful."

"Are you ready to go home?"

"Home? Home?"

"Do you want to go back to our house?" We hadn't discussed anything in a few days that had happened before we left America. Not Stella and not me getting shot. I wanted to take her mind off all that, and start fresh.

"I'm not sure." She tightened her grip on my hand. "I know we have to go back to reality."

"We can go to the penthouse for a few more days when we get back, and then we can go from there."

I had to implement my new business plan in the city, and the penthouse was more secure in terms of keeping her safe. Once people realized I had the backing of Janero, the climate would settle down, and we could return to our home.

"Whatever you think is best," she said. "As long as I'm with you."

"You're always going to be with me."

"These last few days have been amazing." She propped herself on her elbow, letting the sheet slip off her breasts. "I loved being with you. Having you all to myself."

"We can come back here." I traced my finger down her throat and to her breasts. "Whenever you want."

"How about for our anniversary?"

"Anything you want." I swirled my finger around her nipple. "It's yours."

"I think I know what you want." She bit her lip as she crawled on top of me. "You're insatiable."

"I'm not the only one." I pushed my fingers inside her hot, wet pussy. "What should we do about it?"

"I have a few ideas." She swiped her hair away from her face and arched her hips, pushing her breasts forward.

"You're so fucking sexy." I gripped her hips and shifted her over my erection. Her smooth skin almost made me come. "Turn around."

"You always want to be in control." When she turned around, and started to scoot off me, I realized why she thought I wanted her to turn around.

"Where are you going?" I grabbed her arm.

"You said to turn around. I thought you wanted to do it from behind."

"Maybe later." I guided her to straddle my lap with her facing away from me. "I want a view of your ass when you ride me."

She glanced over her shoulder and shot me a devious smirk. "Giddy up." She raised her bottom as I took my cock in my hand and helped her ease down on it. She tensed when I thrust upward.

"You have to move with me. I promise, you're going to love it."

"Okay." Once she relaxed, I was able to moved upward, sheathing myself inside her. "Oh... that's, wow."

"The feeling is mutual." I took her slender waist in my hands, and guided her up and down. We went slow, giving her time to adjust. "That's it, baby."

She placed her hands over mine, losing her initial apprehension. Before long, she took control of the tempo. Bobbing up and down, increasing the pace every few seconds. Her breathing became labored, and her moans were louder.

I glanced at her in the mirror hanging over the dresser. Her eyes were closed and her mouth slightly opened. Her perky tits bounced as her wild hair fell over them. No porn star would ever rival my gorgeous wife.

My balls tightened when she arched her body and leaned back. I twisted my hand in her hair as it brushed along my chest. With a few quick thrusts, she screamed out her pleasure, slowing her pace and coating me in her fresh arousal. I continued to move inside her, but I could tell she was tired from this position.

I guided her off me, and directed her to the edge of the sleigh bed. I got behind her, running my hand down her spine and to her ass.

"It's my turn." With a swift motion, I pulled her hips toward me, and entered her. "Fuck!"

"Romero." She braced herself against the foot of the bed, holding on as I pounded into her.

"Lu!" I yelled. "Baby, this is so good."

"I love you," she panted. "So much."

"I love you."

No truer words were ever spoken. I didn't know it was possible to love anyone as much as I loved her. She calmed me, and gave my brutal soul a purpose. Some days I told myself she was my redemption. When we were together, I could forget who I was, and be her husband. The man she wanted me to be. If only I could be him all the time for her. If only I could give her what she really wanted from me.

"Romero..."

I pulled out of her, and flipped her onto her back.

She stared at me with desperation in her gaze as I spread her legs and slipped inside her. She hooked her legs around my hips as I lowered myself onto her. I kissed her neck, working my way down to her breasts. I licked and swirled my tongue around her nipple, biting down on it, and making her cry out. Trailing my lips along her throat and to her mouth, I kissed her deeply.

We moved as one, in perfect sync. Giving and taking from one another, completing each other. She clenched around my cock, clawing at my back, and thrashing beneath me. I thrust into her one final time, releasing fast and hard. Her head fell to the side as her legs dropped from my waist. She let go around me. Quietly and effortlessly. Making love to her was the most natural thing I had ever experienced.

"Luciana." I gently kissed her.

"Yes," she whispered.

"Fucking you is an absolute pleasure."

"Same." She laughed into the side of my neck. "I'm going to be sore tomorrow."

"It will make you remember what I did to you."

"As if I could forget."

"How about I draw you a bath?" I ran my hand along her side. "I'll get a bottle of champagne for you."

"Will you join me in the tub?"

"You know I'm not a bath kind of guy."

"I was never a 'let's have sex five times in two hours kind of girl', but here we are."

"It was six times, and you loved every second of it."

"Wasn't three and four the same time? You never removed yourself from me."

"I've lost track." I rolled off her, and pulled her to my chest. "It's going to be difficult to leave here tomorrow."

"Back to reality."

"Does that disappoint you?"

"No, I love our life, even if it gets a little crazy."

"A little?"

"I'm going to be okay." She kissed my cheek. "We're going to be okay."

"If it ever gets to be too much, you tell me, and I'll find a way to make it better." I couldn't stop what was happening in my business, but I could control her happiness. "As long as you tell me what you're feeling or thinking, I can make it work."

"That goes two ways." She rested her hand on my chest. "I want to take care of you as much as you want to take care of me. We're in this together."

I hope you mean that.

"Let's get that bath started," I said. "I'll get the champagne once you're in the tub."

"Can we stay like this for a few more minutes?" She hugged me. "This moment is perfect, and I don't ever want to forget it."

"Neither do I."

As much as I wanted it to always be like this, once we got home real life would get in the way. If Gio and I were going to take over the city, the next few months of transition would be uncertain. New alliances would need to be formed. There would be a power struggle. More violence would occur. Our lives might not ever be the same, but everything I did was to protect her.

If I was on top, I had a better chance of keeping her safe. And that was my main goal.

CHAPTER 17

Luciana

Coming back from Italy was difficult. I loved spending time with Romero. We connected and spent so much uninterrupted time together. For the first time in our relationship, we were a married couple. Being back at the penthouse had its challenges. It wasn't as big as our house and there were times when there was no privacy. Between Gio, the guards, and various business associates coming and going at all hours of the day and night, I couldn't get into a routine.

As much as I hated going back to the last place I saw Stella, it was time for Romero and I to go home. We had to move forward with our lives. I wasn't sure what that was going to look like yet, but we had to try. If we were home, maybe I wouldn't constantly feel like the wife of a mafia kingpin. We could get back to some normalcy.

I wandered down the hall to the study. The door wasn't shut, so I figured it was safe to go in and see how my husband was doing, but as I got closer, I could hear Romero and Gio talking. I turned to walk away, but I stopped when I overheard their conversation. I didn't mean to, but I wanted to make sure I understood what they said.

"I'm in the process of setting up the accounts for the offshore money," Gio said. "All of our legitimate staff at Cantinos have been replaced with more reliable people."

"What did you do with the employees who were working there?" Romero asked.

"They've all been relocated. Everyone was taken care of. Santino helped me with that."

Why would they have to replace the employees at the club?

"I can let Janero know we're good to go then?" Romero asked. "We're ready to launder his cash?"

"I don't see why not."

Launder cash? Through the club? That didn't sound very legitimate.

"We're going to have to use the other clubs too," Gio said. "We can't funnel it all through one place. It's too suspicious."

"I figured that." Romero's voice held no surprise. "I want to start conservatively. No red flags. Everything has to appear on the up and up."

Appear on the up and up? Romero and Gio kept discussing their new plan, but all I could focus on was the one safe place I thought we would always have. The club. Why would they compromise an opportunity to get out if they could?

When I turned to leave, I knocked into a small table outside the study, pushing the legs against the floor. It made a loud noise, but I ran up the steps and to the bedroom, hoping no one would realize it was me.

I grabbed a book from the nightstand and jumped on the bed. My heart raced inside my chest when Romero entered the bedroom. He shut the door, and then joined me on the bed. I looked up from the book.

"You overheard my conversation, didn't you?" He took the book from me and tossed it on the bed.

"I didn't mean to."

"I'm running New York City." He stretched his neck to one side, releasing a small crack. "I had to make changes in my organization. Working with Janero was one of them."

"I thought the clubs were off-limits."

"That was before all this other shit happened. I need leverage, and that is what I have to offer."

I traced my finger along the pattern in the comforter, trying to conceal my disappointment.

"You're upset."

"Yeah, I am." I sighed. "I thought as long as you had something legal, maybe one day..." *Why am I even going there?* "I thought things could be different one day."

"I never promised you I would go legit. This is my life. The only life I know." He placed his hand on my thigh. "I want you to be happy. I know that I can't be happy without you."

"What are you saying?"

"I can't walk away." He closed his eyes. "Even if I wanted to. You have to decide if this is the life you want."

"I want a life with you." Why did this have to be so complicated? "I just don't want the danger. I don't like knowing the things you have to do to survive. The deals you make. The ways you have to jeopardize yourself and those around you."

"I protect those around me."

Sometimes...

"I may not tell you everything about my business, but most of what I do has never been a secret." His voice was low, but the tone of this conversation frightened me. "I can't change who I am, Luciana. You can't change who I am."

"You have to let me process what you're doing with the club." I placed my hand on his. "I'm not trying to get in the middle of your business decisions. It's not so much what you're doing with the club that upsets me."

"What upsets you then?"

"It's what the club symbolized to me."

"A way out?"

"For both of us, and Gio too."

"Baby, that was never going to happen."

"In the back of my mind I thought we could get away. Start over." I shrugged. "Be normal. It was a stupid dream, but I wanted to believe it."

"It's a great dream." He squeezed my hand. "But it's not going to happen with me."

Is he giving me permission to walk away?

"I love you, and I'll give you a good life whether you're with me or not." The muscles in his face tensed. "I'll always take care of you, Luciana."

"No." A tear slid down my cheek. "I don't want…no."

"I know, baby." He pressed his lips to mine. "I don't want you to go anywhere. I'll lose my mind without you, but I won't let you lose yours by staying with me. You've been through so much in your life. This is a barbaric way to survive. I can't get out, but if you need to walk, I can do that for you."

I didn't recognize the man standing in front of me.

"It hurts to say that. I've never done anything that good in my life."

"That's not true."

"Am I too much, Lu? Is my world too much?"

I wanted to tell him the truth. There were days when I

was so desperate, I didn't know how I was going to survive. From the time my parents were killed, through my childhood, living with the Torrios, not being able to choose who I wanted to be, and then being forced to marry a man I didn't know. One I thought I could never love. It was all too much.

"Romero," Gio yelled up the stairs. "We're not done down here."

"Fuck," he mumbled.

"You should go." I gently kissed him. "I'm fine."

"No, you're not!" He raised his voice. "You keep saying you are, but I know you're not. How could you be?"

"Why are you upset?"

"You're disappointed in me."

"No, not in you. I'm disappointed with the circumstances." I didn't want to have this conversation. "Let's forget about it. You have to do what you have to do."

"But you'll never understand why I have to do what I have to do." He took my face between his hands. "I'm sorry."

When he stared at me, I wanted to break into a million pieces. I had never seen him look so desperate before. Why did he think I wanted to walk away from him? Why didn't he know I could never leave him?

He caressed my lips with his, kissing me softly. He got up off the bed, and left the room without another word. I went after him, but when I got to the hallway, my phone rang. I could have ignored it, but maybe it was a sign to leave Romero alone for a while.

I glanced at the screen, not recognizing the number, but I answered it anyway. I needed a distraction.

"Hello," I answered.

"Luciana?" I didn't recognize the woman's voice on the other end of the line.

"Yes."

"You don't know me," she said. "You knew my mother."

"Oh?" My stomach dropped when I realized who this could be.

"My name is Carly."

"Stella's daughter?" I went back into the bedroom and closed the door, trying to process that Stella's daughter reached out to me. "How are you?"

That was a stupid question. She was sad and grieving. *Why is she calling me?*

"I'm hanging in there," she said. "I have to ask you for a favor."

"Anything." I would do anything to make up for what had happened to Stella. "What can I do for you?"

"My sisters and I are going through Mom's things and we were looking for her cookbooks. We were wondering if there was any chance that she may have left them at your house?"

"She has taken cookbooks to my house, but I'm not sure if she left any behind."

"Oh." I heard the disappointment in her voice. "Is there any way you can check? We're looking for a special one with her grandmother's recipes."

"I haven't been back to my house since...Well, I'm not home."

"My sisters and I wanted to cook my father's favorite meal my mother always made him, but I need her recipe. It would mean so much to us if you could look for this cookbook. We can't find it anywhere."

"When did you need it?" I asked.

"Today, if possible. We're going grocery shopping tonight," she said. "I could meet you at the house and see if the book is there."

"Ah, you don't have to go to my house." I didn't even want to go to that house. "I could get it and bring it to you."

"That's not a good idea."

Considering what had happened at the funeral, she was probably right.

"This would mean so much to my family," she said. "I don't want to bother you though."

"You're not bothering me," I said. "I can meet you there in about an hour if that works?"

"That would be great, but..." she hesitated. "I hate to ask this."

"What is it?"

"My dad would be furious if he knew that I was going to your house. He doesn't want me anywhere near your husband or his men."

"Well, my husband won't be there." Actually, how was I going to persuade him to let me go?

"What about your guard or other people associated with your husband? I don't want to upset my dad. He's having a difficult time with my mom's death. That's why we want to make this meal for him."

"I understand." I wouldn't be able to get Sam to take me without clearing it with Romero. "I can come alone."

I glanced around the room, looking for my bag, knowing how wrong this was.

"Thank you." I heard the relief in her voice. "I'll meet you at your house. Can you text the location?"

"Sure." I slipped on my shoes, and then quietly left the bedroom. "I'll be there within the hour.

"You're a good person, Luciana. My mom will be so happy when we get that cookbook."

"I hope it's at the house." I unlocked the door at the end of the hall that led to the fire escape.

"Me too."

"See you soon." I gently nudged it open, looking over my shoulder to make sure no one was behind me.

I ended the call, and tossed the phone in my bag. I pressed the door shut, trying not to make any noise. I took a deep breath, knowing what I was attempting was stupid and reckless, but I didn't feel like getting into a fight with Romero. If he even let me go, he would insist that I take Sam with me. He probably would make Sam go and look for the cookbook, and not let me go at all.

I wanted to do this for Stella. Her daughter asked me for something. This might be my only opportunity to do something for her family. All I had to do was go home, look for the book, and give it to Carly. Romero would probably be cooped up in his meeting with Gio, he wouldn't even know I was gone.

When I reached the bottom of the fire escape, I opened the gate, and stepped onto the busy New York sidewalk. As I looked around, I couldn't remember the last time I had been anywhere alone. It was more freeing than I had realized.

I walked along the street and to the parking garage across from the building, where Romero and Gio kept the cars. My heart raced inside my chest because what I was about to do was risky. If I succeeded, I would be able to do this one last thing for Stella.

If my plan failed, Romero would be onto me in about three minutes. If that happened, there would be nowhere for me to escape from his wrath. That was a chance I was willing to take.

For Stella...

CHAPTER 18

Romero

I couldn't focus on my meeting with Gio. I had made the decision to launder the money for Janero. He could handle the details. Maybe I needed to take a step back, and see this from Lu's perspective. It was difficult to read her.

What did she want from me? She knew that I couldn't give up this life. It shouldn't be a choice.

"Rocco is on his way up," Gio said. "He said it was important."

"Fine." I swiveled my chair around and gazed out the window.

Why did I say those things to Luciana? Why did I make her think I would be okay with her walking out of this relationship? That was the last thing I wanted. As if I could let her go. I was far too selfish for that, and I loved her way too much to lose her.

I stood from the chair and headed for the door. I had to handle my personal shit before I could make any more business decisions.

"Where are you going?" Gio asked.

"You can handle Rocco." I reached for the door handle. "I have to go see Lu."

"Romero, get your fucking head in the game," he shouted. "Now is not the time to lose focus. If you and Lu can't get your shit together, you'll have to figure it out later."

"I can't figure it out later," I said. "I have to tell her something now."

When I opened the door, Rocco stood on the other side.

"Hey," he said.

"Hi." I motioned for him to come inside. "Whatever you have to say, Gio can deal with it."

"It's something you need to hear from me." He moved into the study. "You need to hear it now."

"It sounds serious." Gio shut the door. "What's up?"

I leaned against the door, hoping whatever this was could be dealt with quickly, so I could get back to my wife. She was far more important than whatever my new sibling had to say.

"I've been going over the footage you sent from the night Stella was murdered." Rocco ran his hand along his chin. "It's taken me a couple weeks because I needed to be absolutely sure. I had someone I trust help me enhance certain frames in an attempt to get a clearer shot."

"What did you find?" Gio asked. "Anything that can help us identify Stella's killer?"

"Unfortunately, yes," he said. "I think so."

"What does that mean?" I asked. "Do you know who did it?"

Rocco nodded.

"You fucking swore to me it wasn't anyone in your family." I clenched my fist. "Who did this?"

"I didn't think anyone in my family could do this. My

father would not have ordered this." He held his hand up. "What happened in your house had nothing to do with what the rest of us are dealing with. This was personal."

"Who fucking did it?" I shouted. "Just tell me."

"What did you see on the footage?" Gio asked. "Can you give us a positive ID?"

"The footage was grainy, but my guy was able to enhance it enough for me to confirm my suspicions." He lifted his sleeve and showed us a tattoo on the side of his wrist. "The tattoo is my family crest. It dates back decades. My brothers and I all got the symbol tattooed in the same place a few years ago."

"You saw the crest in the footage?" I gritted my teeth. "Vincent?"

"Yes."

"Fuck!" I yelled. "You're sure?"

"More sure than I ever wanted to be." Rocco shook his head. "Even in a mask there was something familiar about the guy in the footage. Once I had a clear image of the tattoo, there was no denying it."

"Is the second person in the footage Sandro?" Gio asked.

"No, Sandro would never do anything like this. His hands are clean. He's never killed anyone. We wouldn't let him."

"You're fucking telling me it was Vincent in that footage?" I should have known it was a Torrio. "You know what I have to do now that I know, and yet you came to me anyway."

I had to make sure this wasn't another trap.

"I've struggled with this decision for a few days," he admitted. "Vincent is my brother, but ever since that night you came for Lu there has been something different about him. He's doing a lot of things without my father's approval. He won't listen to me."

"Did you tell him what you know?" I asked.

"No." Rocco sighed. "He's out of control. He went too far when he murdered an innocent woman. I don't know what else he's capable of."

"Maybe we could issue a warning," Gio said. "Now that we have Janero on our side, he could relocate Vincent. Make sure he doesn't come after anyone else."

"You want me to show mercy?" I glared at Gio. "Did he show mercy when he shot Stella in the head?"

"God." Rocco closed his eyes. "I can't believe this. Why would he do that?"

"Whatever happened," I said. "You'll have clean hands. I'll never tell anyone where this information came from. It stays between the three of us. Your father will never know and neither will Sandro. I owe you that."

"I don't want to be responsible for Vincent's death." He paced the room. "You were eventually going to find out."

"You're not responsible for what happens to him. He did that all on his own. He should have come after me. Instead, he killed an innocent woman." *Fuck!* I should have killed him when he took Luciana. If I had shown no mercy then, Stella would still be alive. "I know this wasn't an easy choice for you, but I won't forget this. I won't forget your loyalty."

"Maybe my father could handle this situation," Rocco said. "Like Gio said, what if we banished him from all the business? What if he sent him away?"

"What if that was just the beginning? What if he comes after me again? What if he hurts Luciana?" I shouted. "He invaded my home. He broke Lu's heart when he murdered Stella."

"Romero," Gio said before being interrupted by the ring of his phone. "It's Jag."

"Jag?" What the hell did he want? "Isn't he supposed to be guarding the downstairs door?"

"Jag," Gio answered. "What's up?"

I sat on the edge of my desk, processing what Rocco had revealed. He had to have known I would retaliate once I learned the truth.

"She did what?" Gio's surprised tone alerted me that we might have a problem. "Are you sure it was her?"

"Who?" I asked.

Gio held up his hand as he listened to Jag. "I don't know," he said. "Hold on a second." He looked at me. "We have a problem."

"What kind of problem?"

"According to Jag, Luciana took one of my cars and headed out of the city. Jag followed her, but there was an accident on the turnpike, and he can't get around it, but she did before they blocked it off."

"What the fuck is he talking about?" I walked to the door, and swung it open. "Luciana," I yelled. "She's upstairs. Why would she take your car? Maybe I hit Jag too hard and he lost some brain cells." *Fucking idiot.* "Lu," I shouted as I walked into the hallway.

Gio and Rocco followed me.

"She's upstairs," I said.

"Are you sure?" Rocco asked.

"That's where I left her." After I told her if she wanted to leave me, I would always take care of her. "Lu!"

Sam came inside from guarding the hallway. "What's going on?"

"Where's Luciana?" I ran up the stairs and to the

bedroom. The door was open, but she wasn't there. "Did she leave here?"

"Not through the front door." Sam joined me in the hall. "I would have seen her."

"The fire escape," Gio said. "If she wanted to leave without being detected."

"Could someone have come in that way?" The thought of her being taken from me again crept into my head.

"Jag said she was alone when she got into my car and drove off." Gio took out his phone. "I'll check the app and see where she's headed."

I didn't wait for him to find her location. I hurried back downstairs and to the study to grab my phone. This woman would be the death of me. How was I supposed to keep her safe if she ran off without telling me?

I called her phone, but it went to voicemail. "Fuck!"

"She's probably driving and can't pick up," Rocco said.

"She picks now to be safe?" I called her phone again. "Did you get her location?"

"I don't think you're going to like it," Gio said.

"If I have to go get her from your house, Rocco, I will leave no one standing this time," I shouted. "Where is she?"

"Your house." Gio showed me his phone. "She's pulling onto the street now."

"Why would she go home?" I called her phone again. "This doesn't make any fucking sense. What is she doing?"

"Hello," she answered in a soft voice. "Don't be mad."

"Don't be mad? Are you out of your damn mind? Why are you at our house? Why would you fucking go alone?"

"I said don't be mad."

"Luciana? I am mad, so just tell me what you're doing."

"Stella's daughter called me and asked if I could get her mom's cookbook."

"We could have sent someone to get it."

"She said her dad didn't want her around you or any of your guys. I'm meeting her here to get the book. I'll be in and out, and then I'll be right home."

"Why did you sneak out of the house?"

"Would you have let me come?"

"No." I rubbed my temple.

"I'm sorry, I just…"

"Get in that car and get back here," I shouted. "I'm not fucking around."

"Romero, I need to do this."

She wasn't thinking of the emotional distress this was going to put her in if she went into the kitchen alone. She could have a panic attack. I didn't want her there by herself.

"I'll be fine," she said. "I'm going into the house now."

"Which daughter called you?"

"Carly."

"How did she get your number?"

"I don't know. Maybe from Stella's phone."

"She told you to come without me or a guard?" This didn't sound right. "How did she even know the book was in our house?"

"I don't know, but she can't find it. It's logical that it would be in our kitchen. Stella was teaching me her recipes."

"Lu, get in the car, lock the doors, and come back here." I glanced at Gio. "Forget about the book. Don't go in the house."

"I'm already in the house."

"Get out of the fucking house now!"

"Romero, I'm…Ouch!" She screamed, then the phone sounded like it hit the ground.

"Lu? What happened?"

"What's wrong?" Gio asked.

"The phone... it sounded like she dropped it. We got disconnected." I ended the call, and then dialed her back, but it went straight to voicemail. "What the fuck?"

"She's at your house?" Rocco took out his phone. "I can have some of my guys from my house go to yours to check on her. They can get there faster than you can."

"The same guys who held a gun on us a few months ago? How do I know they can be trusted?" I shook my head because I didn't trust the Torrios.

"He's right," Gio said. "Given what you just told us about Vincent, we can't trust your people."

"I'm going to the house now," I said. "This is a nightmare."

"Jag said there was an accident. It's going to take us a while to get there."

"What am I supposed to do? She walked into a fucking trap. I know she did." I grabbed my gun from the desk drawer. "Gather up our guys. Call Jag and see if he got past the accident."

"I want to go with you," Rocco said. "No matter what you think of me, Lu is my family. I don't want anything to happen to her."

"If anything happens to her..." I closed my eyes, and took a breath. "Nothing better happen to her or I will fucking lose my shit."

CHAPTER 19

Luciana

"Lu, get in the car, lock the doors, and come back here." Romero grew more agitated with each word. I was going to be in a lot of trouble for this, but something told me I had to do it. "Forget about the book. Don't go in the house."

"I'm already in the house."

After I hit the code in for the security system, the quietness startled me. There was always someone in the house. The guys would say hello when I came in. Romero and Gio were usually in the study fighting over something stupid. There was no life left in this house.

Once I entered the foyer, I froze as I looked around. The last time I was here...*Stella.*

My heart ached as an unsettled sensation came over me.

"Get out of the fucking house now!" Romero snapped.

A tingle ran down my spine as I headed down the hallway to the kitchen, but as long as Romero stayed on the phone with me, I could do this.

"Romero, I'm...Ouch!" The pressure around my arm

caused me to drop the phone. When I looked to my right, I realized Romero's instincts had been correct. "Vincent."

"I'm so glad you could join me, Lu." He increased the pressure on my arm as he crushed my phone under the weight of his foot. "We have some unfinished business." He yanked me down the hall and to the kitchen.

"Stop it!" I struggled against him. "What do you want?"

"Stella's cookbook." He laughed. "Can you get it for me?"

"You? It wasn't her daughter?" I pulled out of his hold. "Why would you do that?" I thought for a moment, trying to figure out what was going on. "How did you even know about the cookbook?"

"Which question do you want me to answer first?" He straightened his tie. He looked as if he had come right from the law firm. Not a hair out of place or a crease that didn't belong in his suit.

"Why am I doing this or how did I know about the cookbook? You're a smart girl, Luciana, well except when it comes to husbands, but I guess that really isn't your fault. You can't figure out how I knew about the cookbook?"

"What do you want?" I shouted.

"Look." He grabbed me by the back of my hair and forced me into the kitchen. My legs shook and my stomach churned just like the night I found Stella lying in her own blood. Lifeless, pale, and dead. "The cookbook is right where Stella left it." He pointed to the counter by the stove. "Did you enjoy your cooking lessons?"

"How did you know about that book?" I tried to create some space between us, but the more I struggled, the harder he held my hair. "You've never been here before."

"Haven't I?" He shoved me against the counter. "What do I want? I want your piece of shit husband to suffer for the devastation he has brought down on my family."

"What are you talking about?"

"Ever since he came into our lives, we've had nothing but problems. We were thriving as the lead mafia family before him. Now, we can't move our products."

"That's not his fault."

"How would you know? Does he discuss his business with you?"

"No, but your family went after him, and I was there for that. Anything he had to do to retaliate should have been expected."

"That might have been true from a business standpoint."

When he glared at me, I couldn't find any traces of the man I used to know. He had always frightened me, but I never really thought he would hurt me. Even when he held me hostage a few months ago, I didn't believe he would harm me, but I didn't have that confidence today. I didn't believe he would let Romero have another shot at saving me.

I would have to save myself this time.

"If this isn't about business, what is it about?" I eyed the knives inside the wooden block on the counter. "What are you trying to get back at Romero for?"

"That man has destroyed my family." When he walked around the kitchen island, I inched closer to the knives. "My mother left, my father is not as powerful as he once was, and Rocco...fuck! I don't even know who he is. He was a Torrio and now..."

"That's not Romero's fault." I backed up until I was in front of the knives. "That was your mother's secret. She destroyed your family."

"But your husband helped reveal that secret."

"Because you backed him into a corner. If you didn't

take me that day, Romero wouldn't have had to come for me. Once you realized your alliance wasn't going to work, you should have left us alone. Your family is the one who screwed up. You went after a man you couldn't bring down."

"*My* family? You're a Torrio too."

"Now I'm a Torrio? When it's convenient for you? I was never part of your family until you needed me to marry Romero." My heart raced with anticipation. Each time he turned away from me, I made a move for a knife, but he would quickly turn back around, leaving me no choice but to abandon my plan. "I'm a Bilotti."

"Then we'll make sure that's what it says on your headstone. If I have my way, they will put the word *traitor* under it."

"I'm not a traitor." I clenched my fist. "I chose the right side."

"You chose the side that will get you killed." He paced the kitchen. "Because of you, I've lost everything. Your husband is making a power play that will destroy my family's reign. Romero needs to feel the pain of losing you. That will be the only way I'll bring him down."

"He'll become more ruthless than ever if you kill me. He'll never stop coming for you."

"Not if he doesn't know it was me who did it. All I want to do is break him, and then bring him down. I'll succeed where my father couldn't. I'll be the one to end him, and take my rightful place at the top. I will not allow Romero to take control of the city."

"He's smart. He'll figure out it was you."

"Like he figured out what happened in his own house?" He ran his hand through his hair. "You had to flee to the penthouse because your strong, powerful husband couldn't stop an attack in his own house, much less figure out who the hell the attacker is."

"What are you saying?" I glanced at the cookbook as a harsh revelation came over me. "You have been here before."

"I knew you could figure it out." A grin crossed his smug, twisted face. "See, you are a smart girl. Too bad you're never going to become that attorney you so desperately want to be."

"Stella? No." I closed my eyes, fighting back the tears. "I don't believe you're capable of that."

"You don't know me very well, do you?" He leaned against the island, with his back toward me. "Of course, I didn't expect Stella to be here that night."

A burning sensation took over my body. Something that I had never experienced before.

Is this rage? I was blinded by it. Almost as if a white, painful light flashed in front of me. All I could think about was grabbing the knife and plunging it deep inside him.

"She was an added bonus." He relaxed his stance as he spoke of that night. He was too casual. Like her life didn't matter. "I thought I would take out a guard or two as a warning. I figured a breach in Romero's security system would be enough to throw him off balance."

"Why?" That night all came back to me. My chest tightened and I couldn't catch my breath. "Why her?"

"Stella was on her way in the house with your birthday cake." He tilted his head to the side. "I was overlooked on the guest list for your party the night before. Rocco and Sandro weren't."

"She was innocent. She had a family. You didn't have to hurt her."

"She was in the wrong place at the wrong time." He

sighed. "But once she saw us, I had to take advantage of the situation. I had to use her presence as an opportunity."

"You're an animal." My body shook when I thought about how scared Stella must have been as she faced her attacker. Being in this house made her a target.

"No more than your husband or Rocco or Gio." He shrugged. "We all do what we have to do. I had to shoot Stella. I had to make Romero suffer."

I took a deep breath, trying to think like a rational person, but it was as if I wasn't myself. With his confession, I stepped outside of my body. Nothing mattered but getting justice for Stella. In that moment, I finally understood who I was, and where I had come from. My family's world, Romero's world made sense.

"She knew her fate, Lu." He laughed. "She was brave too. She told me to go fuck myself right before I pulled the trigger and blew out her brains."

I didn't remember grabbing the knife as I ran around the island and lunged toward him. When the blade connected with the front of his shoulder, I pushed it in as he screamed out in agony.

"You fucking bitch."

"No!" I let go of the knife, still embedded in his flesh, as he came toward me.

"I was going to make your death quick, but now you're going to pay." He gritted his teeth and removed the knife from his shoulder, screaming like an injured animal caught in a trap. I ran to the back door, and tugged on the handle. *Locked*! I turned the brass lock, but he slammed his hand against the door, preventing me from opening it.

"Leave me alone!" I screamed.

"I'll leave you alone when you're dead." When he

reached for his gun, I punched his bleeding shoulder, knocking him back. "Fuck!"

I hustled down the hall, slamming into Jag on my way out.

"Jag?" I pushed him toward the door. "We have to get out of here."

"Are you okay?" He lowered his gun, and looked me over. "Are you hurt?"

"No, but how did you find me? Is Romero here?" I reached for the door. "We have to get out of here. Vincent is here and he's lost his mind."

"Let's go," he said. "The car is…ahh!"

"Jag?" I screamed when a loud firecracker sound vibrated off the walls, and then he fell to the floor. "No, no," I dropped to my knees. "Jag?"

"Get up." Vincent grabbed me by my hair and flung me into the staircase, knocking the wind out of me.

"What did you do?"

"What do you think I did?" He waved his gun in front of me. "You're next."

I scrambled to my feet, holding onto the banister, trying to get my footing.

"I'm not going to make it painless." He shoved me back, causing me to fall on the steps.

When he came for me, I kicked him as hard as I could where I had stabbed him.

"Fuck! You bitch."

As he staggered away from me, I got to my feet and ran up the stairs, and to my bedroom. I turned to shut the door, but he was already up the steps and coming toward me, aiming his gun at me. Slamming the door shut, I locked it as quickly as I could. I reached in my pocket to grab my phone, but then I remembered Vincent had smashed it.

"Luciana!" He pounded on the door, causing me to jump. He began kicking the door, shaking it from the frame. It was only a matter of seconds before he busted it open. "I hope your short-lived marriage with your scumbag husband was worth your life."

As he gave the door one final kick, I snagged the large crystal vase from the dresser. When he came through the door, I advanced him as fast as I could and smacked him in the head with it. The impact was hard enough to make him lose his balance and drop his gun.

He stumbled into the hall, pressing his hand against his head. Blood gushed from the gash.

I moved forward, trying to retrieve the gun, but he came at me, taking me down to the floor. I kicked and thrashed, rolling myself onto my stomach. He yanked my head back by my hair as I stretched as far as I could. My fingertips grazed the gun, but I couldn't get it.

He let go of my hair, and wrapped his hand around my throat. In that second, I scooted forward enough to grab the gun. When he squeezed my throat, I scratched at his arm with my free hand, all the while trying to get a better grasp on the weapon. Once I had it, I tossed my hand back, and hit him in the face with it. He lost his hold on my throat, giving me the opportunity to crawl away from him, and get into a seated position.

This time when he came for me, I shouted, "Stop!"

My hand trembled as I pointed the gun at him, but I would shoot him.

His eyes widened when he realized I had the upper hand.

"What are you going to do with that?" He wiped the blood from his head. "Give it to me." He held out his hand.

"You're not going to shoot me. You don't even know how to use it."

"Do you want to bet on that?" I pushed myself off the floor, trying to steady my hand as I put my finger on the trigger. "Stay down."

"Lu, this isn't a game." He held up his hand. "You're trembling. Put the gun down."

"You deserve to die after what you did to Stella." The tears streamed down my face. "I won't let you hurt anyone else. You're never going to hurt me again." A violent shudder coursed through me, and I wasn't sure how much longer my legs would hold me up.

He tried to stand, but I stepped toward him. "Don't move." My rocky hand almost caused me to drop the gun. "I never wanted to be part of this world. I wanted to go away to school. Your family used me as a pawn in a twisted game. I didn't want any of this," I shouted. "But you forced me into this life. Now you're going to suffer the consequences."

"Lu, you don't know what you're saying." He stretched out his arm. "You're not going to shoot me. Think about Rocco and Sandro. You can't shoot me. You don't have it in you."

"He's right, Luciana." Romero came up from behind me, and placed his hand on mine, steadying my hold on the gun. "You don't have it in you to shoot him, but I sure as fuck do."

"Romero." I collapsed against his chest, never more relieved to see him. "He killed Stella. He shot her," I sobbed. "It was him."

"I know, baby." He slowly took the gun from my hand, never taking the aim away from Vincent. "I'm here. It's all right."

"I'm sorry I... Jag." I pointed toward the hall. "He shot Jag too."

"Jag is okay." He guided me to the doorway. "I need you to go with Gio now. He's going to take you downstairs."

"No, I don't want to leave you with him," I cried. "He killed Stella."

"I'm going to be fine, butterfly." He stared down at Vincent. "You let me handle this."

"Fuck you," Vincent said. "Just pull the trigger."

"Lu." Gio put his arm around me. "Let's go downstairs."

"Gio." I rested my head on his shoulder. "I thought Stella's daughter called me. I didn't know it was..."

"We know, beauty." He nodded at Romero before leading me into the hallway. "I got you."

When we got to the bottom of the steps, Salvi applied pressure to Jag's arm. Rocco and Joey stood in the doorway, as the other guards moved around the front of the property. The scene appeared calm and normal. Not all like the chaos one would expect for the scenario unfolding in front of us.

"Jag." I dropped down beside him. "Are you okay?"

"I'm fine." He smiled. "Sorry I didn't get to you in time."

"It's okay. You came for me." I took his hand. "I'm sorry you got hurt. That was my fault."

When the loud, unmistakable sound of the gun went off from upstairs, my gaze connected with Rocco's. We knew what it meant. Gio put his hand on my shoulder, and gave it a gentle squeeze. No one said anything.

It was business as usual.

CHAPTER 20

Romero

"Fuck!" Vincent said in a weak voice after the bullet shot into his thigh.

He gazed up at me in disbelief. Did he really think I missed?

"That's right," I said. "You're still alive."

"What are you doing?" He coughed up blood. "Just get it over with."

"You want me to make this quick for you? You don't want me to make you suffer?"

"Fuck you." He gritted through the pain. "Just kill me."

"There's one reason you're not dead." I walked around his battered body. "Looks like my wife fought hard."

"I didn't think she had it in her." His face twisted in pain, but he still managed a strained laugh. "Poor, weak Lu. She's not as helpless as I thought. Although, you have to work on her instincts. She's an accident waiting to happen."

"I should blow your brains out." I waved the gun over him when I thought about how he terrorized my wife. "With your own gun."

"Why don't you?"

"I told you there's *one* reason you're alive."

"Don't keep me in suspense."

"Rocco," I said. "You're alive because of him. He can decide what to do with your useless ass."

"You would do that for him?"

"He has Bilotti blood running through his veins. I can't deny that."

If Rocco and I were ever going to establish a connection and become true brothers, I couldn't murder Vincent. As much as I hated the situation, it was the cold, hard truth. I wanted to avenge Stella, but I had to look at the bigger picture.

"If you ever come after my wife again, it won't matter who your brother is. I'll kill the rest of your family and make you watch before I shove a gun in your mouth and blow your head off."

He closed his eyes, and breathed through the pain.

"Don't make me keep that promise." I kicked him in the ribs.

"Fuck!"

"That was for Lu." When I kicked him a second time, he screamed out in agony. "That one was for Stella."

I left him bleeding and broken on the bedroom floor.

When I went out into the hallway, I leaned against the wall. My blood raced with adrenaline. I had never shown that kind of restraint before. A huge part of me wanted to walk back in there and kill him. I wanted to be done with him. But if I killed him, it would never be over. Our families were more connected than I liked. I had to look to the future. I would have to make the Torrios pay for what they had done to me in other ways.

I would get creative.

I headed to the staircase, noting how quiet it was in the foyer. There was movement, but no one spoke. When I got to the bottom of the stairs, everyone stared at me.

"Romero." Lu got up from the floor and took my hand. "We heard the, um...well, we didn't know if..."

"I didn't kill him." I looked at Rocco. "He's not dead."

"What?" Rocco moved toward me. "Vincent is alive?"

He tried not to display his relief, but I saw it in his expression. I didn't begrudge him that.

"I did that for you because you're my brother. I showed mercy because you're my blood. I protect my own. You gave me your loyalty today, and I won't forget that."

"I don't know what to say." He gazed up the staircase. "Thank you."

"Vincent is your responsibility. It's up to you what you do with him next, but it's also your responsibility to make sure he never comes at me again, because if he does, there won't be a second chance for either of you. Brother or not."

"I understand."

"You better get to him before he bleeds out on my bedroom floor." I handed him Vincent's gun. "Don't give that back to him today."

He nodded, taking the gun from me.

"We're good." I patted his back, knowing we had plenty of shit to work through, but we would get there. "Go see him."

As Rocco climbed the steps, I took a look at Jag. His face was pale, and his eyes were bloodshot, but he was sitting up and alert.

"How are you?" I asked.

"I've been better, but I'll survive," he said.

"Brett is on his way," Gio informed me. "We're keeping him busy."

"Why don't you ask Rocco what he wants to do with the scumbag upstairs?" I sighed. "I don't need him dying in here."

"I'm sure he'll bring his men in and they can figure out what to do. It sounds like Vincent might have to go to the hospital. I'll advise them to say he was attacked elsewhere, and they took him right to the emergency room. No witnesses. That sort of thing."

"I know you can handle it." I looked at Jag again. "You did good."

If he hadn't seen Luciana get into Gio's car and act as quickly as he did, we might not have known Lu was even missing until it was too late.

"It's my job to protect Lu." Jag smiled at her. "Next time, you should let me drive."

"There won't be a next time." I squeezed Lu's hand as I guided her through the family room, and out the patio door. "What the fuck were you thinking?"

"I wasn't? I acted on instinct."

"Your instincts fucking suck." Her clothes were stained in blood. "Are you bleeding?" I frantically look over her white blood-stained shirt. Everything had been so crazy, I didn't even ask how she was. "Are you hurt?"

"It's not my blood. Well, not all of it." She inspected her bloody hands. "It's Vincent's."

"What happened?"

"I stabbed him with a kitchen knife, and I threw a vase at his head."

"I knew you were a badass."

"I'm a Bilotti."

Her voice bursted with pride, and I couldn't have been prouder of her.

"Yes, you are." I tugged her close to me, wrapping my

arms around her waist. "That's why you can never do what you did today ever again. You walked right into a trap. This isn't the first time that's happened. You're a target because you're my wife."

"I know."

"I'm so glad you're alive and he didn't hurt you, but I'm furious with you."

"How furious?"

"Furious enough to make you a prisoner. From now on, you don't leave my side. And when I have to leave your side, you will be under lock and key with ten guards surrounding you."

"I think that's extreme."

"I don't care what you think." I held her tight. "That's not true. I care about your thoughts and your feelings. I care whether you are hurt. I don't want to be the one who hurts you. I don't want you to get hurt because of me."

"My family set all of this in motion long before you and I ever met."

"But it didn't end then. The feud continues. The violence won't end."

That was a grim reality for men like me. For men like Vincent, Gio, Rocco, and Sandro. As long as there was power to be had, we would keep fighting to stay on top.

"You stopped fighting with Rocco."

"Because he's my brother."

"But it's a start." She pressed her hand to my cheek. "You could have killed Vincent."

"I wanted to kill him."

"So did I." She looked down. "I never felt that kind of rage before. When he told me he was the one who killed Stella, I wanted to make him suffer."

"I'm glad you didn't kill him, Luciana." I tilted her chin

so she had to look at me. "I don't want that for you. I don't want you to ever know the burden you would carry for ending someone's life."

"I'm grateful that you got here in time. I was so upset. I could have pulled the trigger."

"I would have gotten you through that, but it's better we don't have to."

"Earlier today, you said you would let me go if this life was too much."

"Did I?" *Why is she bringing that up now?* Was today the final straw? Was it too much for her?

"Maybe not in those exact words, but I knew what you were trying to say." She took my hand and grazed my knuckles with her lips. "Did you mean it?"

"Are you asking if I'm ready to set my butterfly free?"

She nodded.

"I'm possessive, and I've always taken what I wanted. I didn't care about the consequences. I did what was right for me." I ran my fingers through her hair. "Then I met you. It took me a while to realize that when I'm with you, I'm not the man I thought I was. I'm still ruthless, and brutal, but I'm different than I was before I married you."

"Do you like the man you became?"

"I like the man I am when I'm with you. You made me that man. The one who loves you with all his heart and soul. I would never make you stay in a life you didn't want." As much as I hated to admit that, I couldn't hurt her. "You married me out of obligation. You weren't given a choice. Even when I found out that you betrayed me, I didn't let you go. I didn't give you a choice."

Her eyes filled with tears.

"You should have a choice, Luciana. As I said earlier, I will always take care of you. It would destroy me if you didn't want to be my wife, but I would respect your decision."

"You've come a long way from the beast who ripped my dress off in the back of a car at our engagement party." She wiped the tears from her cheeks. "I was terrified of you."

"Who wouldn't be?"

"I didn't think we'd last a week, but I was wrong. Even when you found out what I had done, I didn't want to leave you. I appreciate you respecting what I want. I love that you want to give me a choice, but I've already made my decision."

"You have?" It would tear me down if she left me. Who would I become without her?

"Your butterfly does not want to be set free."

"Thank God." I hugged her. "But for the record, even if I did let you go, I'd make you wear an ankle monitor."

"You're the most romantic man I've ever met." She rolled her eyes. "I love you."

"I love you too." I brushed my lips along hers. "I'm going to work to restore peace among the families. I don't want anyone to ever feel the grief of losing someone like Stella ever again. That never should have happened. I didn't kill Vincent for that, but it doesn't mean he won't pay in other ways. I will never forget what he has done to you."

"The less I know, the better off I'll be." She gently kissed me. "But now you know I can handle myself. I'm not afraid to stab a bitch."

"Yeah, that's not happening again." I slowly kissed her, taking my time to relish in her warmth "You're strong, smart, and capable of anything you set your mind to. I'm in absolute awe of you." I ran my tongue along the seam of her mouth. "Stay with me."

"Forever."

I let go of her and took her hands in mine, thankful that after everything we had been through, she still wanted to be with me.

"I appreciate everything you said, but I don't have any intention of leaving you." She rested her head on my shoulder. "I don't like your job. I'm disappointed that you have to use the club for illegal activity. I'm scared every time you leave the house. I'll never get the image of you coming through the door bleeding from that gunshot wound."

"Lu." I wanted to give her a better life.

"Let me finish." She touched my lips with her finger. "I can't live without you. I can handle your world because I want to be with you, but you can't die on me."

"Baby, I'm not going anywhere." I kissed her. "Not as long as I have you to come home to."

"I'm not going anywhere either." She flipped over her wrist and showed me her tattoo. "I'm yours."

I put my arm next to her wrist, lining up our matching tattoos. "And I'm yours."

Today, tomorrow, and forever.

The End

I hope you enjoyed Romero and Luciana's journey. This won't be the last of them. You'll be able to catch up with them in both Gio's book and Rocco's book. Sign up for my newsletter so you don't miss any details about these intriguing upcoming releases.

https://view.flodesk.com/pages/5eaf17b582272f0026fed03a

ABOUT THE AUTHOR

USA Today Bestselling author Ella Jade has been writing for as long as she can remember. As a child, she often had a notebook and pen with her, and now as an adult, the laptop is never far away. The plots and dialogue have always played out in her head, but she never knew what to do with them. That all changed when she discovered the eBook industry. She started penning novels at a rapid pace and now she can't be stopped.

Ella resides in New Jersey with her husband, two boys, and two feisty Chihuahua writing companions. She can often be found creating sexy, domineering men and the strong women who know how to challenge them in and out of the bedroom. She hopes you'll get lost in her words.

Sign up for her newsletter here:

https://view.flodesk.com/pages/5eaf17b582272f0026fed03a

Printed in Great Britain
by Amazon